Three Bird Summer

Three Bird Summer

Sara St. Antoine

CANDLEWICK PRESS

Copyright © 2014 by Sara St. Antoine

First paperback edition 2018

Library of Congress Catalog Card Number 2013946623
ISBN 978-0-7636-6564-7 (hardcover)
ISBN 978-1-5362-0045-4 (paperback)

18 19 20 21 22 23 BVG 10 9 8 7 6 5 4 3 2 1

Printed in Berryville, VA, U.S.A.

This book was typeset in Minion Pro.

Candlewick Press
99 Dover Street
Somerville, Massachusetts 02144

visit us at www.candlewick.com

To Robin

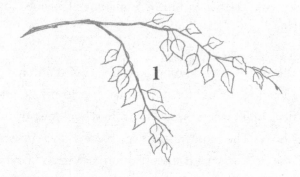

1

HERE'S WHAT I KNOW about girls. They like talking and combing their hair with their fingers, and they move in careful packs, like wolves. They smell like soap and bees. They speak at two volumes: megaphone loud and impossible-to-hear whisper. Even when they're huddled together in hushed conversations, they keep their eyes trained outward, scoping the scene like Secret Service agents. I'm pretty sure they can communicate telepathically, too. They often dress exactly alike — showing up one day all in jean jackets and another day in ruffled skirts and flip-flops — as if they have access to the same secret dress code. In class, they keep their eyes on the teacher, but they can actually see in every direction. I'm sure of it. If you scratch your armpit or put your finger anywhere near your nose, you'll set off a round of giggles. Girls shriek, and they laugh over the smallest things. Words, even. *Prune. Waddle. Unruly.* I hardly ever get what's funny. Sometimes I'm not even sure they do.

On the first day of summer vacation, my mom and I were loading the car for our annual trip to my grandmother's cabin when three girls from school rode by on their bikes. The moment they spotted me, they turned into the driveway with the precision of a team of Blue Angels and came to a stop inches from the car. Today's dress code was short shorts and nail polish the color of root beer.

"Going someplace?" asked Emma. She always talked first.

"Yeah," I said.

"Where?" asked Margaret, glancing skeptically at my hole-pocked sneakers.

"To see my grandma," I said.

The girls laughed. As usual, I had no idea why.

I looked at my mom, but she was too focused on her perfect packing job to get involved. She shoved my duffel against the cooler, then realigned it for maximum efficiency. Next she scooped up two of her work bags and balanced them carefully on top.

"I think that's everything but my purse," she told me. "I'll call Grandma and let her know we're on our way. Don't touch a thing."

She nodded at the girls and headed into the house.

"Where does your grandmother live?" asked Annie, the smallest and the nicest of the three.

"She's at her cabin up north in Minnesota," I said. "On a lake. In the woods."

"Cool," Annie said.

Emma and Margaret were now peering into the back of the car, appraising its contents. Even though there was nothing in there out of the ordinary, I felt weirdly exposed, like they had X-ray vision and could see straight through the fabric of my duffel to my striped boxers, my robot pajamas.

"Are you staying all summer?" Margaret asked.

"Pretty much," I said.

"Who's going to water your roses?" asked Annie, leaning down to sniff our flower bushes.

I stared at her incredulously. Was she really wondering about that? Were all girls just moms waiting to get their promotions? I almost said, "My dad will come by sometimes," but that would have invited a whole new set of questions. So instead I told her I didn't know.

3

They looked at me like I was supposed to say something else. When I didn't, they glanced at one another and exchanged a wordless message. Possible translation: "He's boring. Let's go to Dairy Queen and talk about penmanship."

"Well, have fun!" said Emma, shoving off.

"Watch out for bears!" said Margaret.

Annie just waved.

I heard them laughing as they rode away.

When they turned the corner, I leaned against the car and gazed up at the sky. Sixteen starlings were perched on a set of telephone wires above the street, twitching and fidgeting in the morning air. They clung to the wires in an up-and-down pattern like notes on one of my trumpet scores.

"*Brum, brum, barum,*" I hummed through my lips, imagining the tune. "*Brum brum brum barum.*"

"I sure hope you won't be making noises like that all the way to Minnesota," my mom said, emerging from the house with her purse, a box of Kleenex, and a travel mug. She was wearing a linen skirt and gold sandals that looked right for Wilmette but would be completely out of place at the cabin. She bit her lip and tucked her things into the car. "How did Grandma sound when you two spoke last week?" she asked.

"I don't know. Fine, I guess."

"You think so?" She walked to the back of the car for one final inspection, then slammed the hatch. "Anyway, she had some news. Apparently there are new neighbors on the lake — where the Parkers used to live. They have a girl your age. Grandma says she's darling."

"Grandma actually used the word 'darling'?" I asked. What I didn't say was that the idea of a neighbor girl filled me with dread. Being at the cabin was my chance to get away from Emma, Margaret, Annie, and their kind. I'd be more comfortable encountering a real wolf on Grandma's property than a stray member of the girl pack.

"Well, maybe she said 'cute,'" Mom admitted.

"Which is a word she uses to describe earthworms," I pointed out. "And featherless baby birds with those big bulging eyeballs."

Mom ignored me. "I just thought it might be nice to have someone your age around. With your cousins away and all."

"I don't care about that," I told her. This year, for the first time ever, it would just be me, Mom, and Grandma at the cabin. My parents had gotten divorced over the winter, and this meant that my dad and his side of the family wouldn't be visiting. I hadn't thought much about what it would be like to be the only kid, except that it would be a relief not to have my cousins flipping me out

5

of the hammock in surprise attacks or challenging me to brutal games of chicken on Grandma's canoe. No cousins also meant more pie . . . for me.

"Well, then forget what I said," Mom told me. "It's not like we see a lot of the neighbors when we're up in Grandma's little wilderness anyway."

I slid into the passenger seat and pulled on my seat belt. I really hoped she was right.

2

THERE WAS A MOMENT on the drive to Grandma's cabin when you realized you were finally up north. After counting hay bales for mile after mile of flat farm fields, wondering how long it would take for somebody to invent human teleporting so you would never have to make this boring drive again, you'd suddenly see them: pine trees. Their triangular tops rose up over the horizon — a boundary, a front, a promise — like spindly giants in pointy hats, signaling the beginning of the great North.

Now, even in the near-darkness, I could see the familiar silhouette of the pines as we drove up the two-lane highway toward the town of Hubbard Falls. I rolled my window all the way down and let the night air rush against my face. Warm, then cool; sweet, then skunky.

We skirted the edge of town and followed one last mile of country road to get to Grandma's property. Only a small mailbox on the right side of the road indicated the presence of any kind of human habitation to our left. The woods were dark, and the drive was just a narrow gap between the trees. Mom turned in and drove carefully with her high beams on. We steered around trees and bumped over roots and ruts for nearly half a mile until the cabin appeared, nestled on a rise, with just one exterior light on.

Mom parked our car beside Grandma's old Ford station wagon, and we climbed out into the night. It was too dark to see anything except the small area illuminated by the light, but the smell of pines and damp earth was enough to know we'd made it. I loved arriving at night, when the property felt at its most mysterious, when crazy little bugs whipped through the air and unknown creatures snapped branches beneath the distant trees. But part of what I loved, too, was knowing that when I woke up, the curtain of darkness would be lifted and my summer world would be there, waiting for me.

I slammed the car door, and the sound echoed in the silence.

"Shhh! I'm sure she's asleep by now," Mom whispered.

We pulled our most essential bags from the car and headed up the steps to the cabin. A crowd of moths and june bugs was going nuts around the porch light, slamming against the bulb like hockey players hitting the boards. In the morning, we'd find fried ones scattered among the brown pine needles on the steps below.

Inside the cabin, Mom turned on a light, casting the kitchen in a yellow glow and turning the windows into impenetrable black squares. Two biscuits and a few slices of ham sat in a tin pie plate on top of the stove. Beside them was a small note written in my grandmother's shaky hand, with a pencil beside it:

Thought you said you'd be here by dinner. Eat up.

"I told her we'd be on the late side!" Mom said, sounding exasperated. She took up the pencil and wrote *Sorry!* We both knew Grandma would wake up hours before us, still bothered by our delay.

"Tell her it's because of your coffee habit," I whispered.

"Shhh," she said back.

"Explain how you needed five stops for caffeine and ten stops to pee," I added. Because it was true. I was convinced we'd added two hours to our travel time pulling over at rest areas and gas stations.

"Adam, enough!" my mother whispered. "I'm sure she isn't interested in the gory details. Anyway, it's time for bed."

Mom lingered in the kitchen while I hauled my duffel through the main part of the cabin, breathing in the familiar smell of wood paneling and fireplace cinders. Everything was in its usual place. There were the couches with their lumpy orange cushions, the handmade wooden tables, the bronze reading lamps. There was the Three Bird Lake banner — a large felt rectangle featuring an eagle, a loon, and a great blue heron — hanging over the fireplace as it had for decades. There were the faded books on the shelves, sharing space with collections of rocks, feathers, and pinecones. There were the curled sketches thumbtacked to the walls — crayon drawings my cousins and I had made when we were little, and a few pencil drawings by my grandmother of birds and plants.

Back in my small bedroom, the decor hadn't been changed for decades, either. My bed had a scratchy wool blanket, red with a single black stripe. A small dresser stood against the wall, with an old framed mirror above it. Stuck into the mirror were black-and-white snapshots of my mother as a young girl, a 1961 postcard from Chicago, and a picture of me from kindergarten. Grandma kept a white lacy fabric on top of the dresser at all times, and when I used to tell my mom that it was too girly, she told me to hush and feel grateful that I had my own space at all. My cousins had always had to sleep on pull-out bunks in the main part of the cabin, listening to each other snore.

I dropped my duffel, and it hit the wooden floor with a thud.

"Shhh," my mother said from the hall.

In past summers, that would have been the cue for Dad to tell her to relax. I sighed and pulled on my pajamas.

In the morning, I woke to the sounds of motorboats crossing the lake and the smell of bacon. Grandma made pancakes and bacon for breakfast every morning. It was one of her best traditions.

I got up and made my bed, knowing Mom and Grandma would tolerate nothing less. Then I walked into the living room. All along one side of the cabin, tall windows looked out toward the lake. This was the first thing anyone noticed stepping into the cabin — how it was almost like a giant screened porch. Today I could see patches of blue sky through the tree limbs, and sunlight skipping on Three Bird Lake below.

"Here's Adam!" Mom said as I shuffled into the kitchen.

Grandma was leaning over the stove, plucking bacon from the griddle. She was wearing her usual cabin attire: an oxford shirt rolled up at the sleeves, khaki pants, and little white sneakers. At my mother's words, she turned and looked up — at me and beyond me, it seemed. I looked over my shoulder to see if I was missing something.

"He's grown, hasn't he?" Mom said. "I think he finally has us beat."

Grandma blinked and nodded. She came over and gave me a little kiss on the cheek, then returned to the stove. She jabbed at the remaining bacon with her fork like a bird pecking at worms.

"I see you didn't eat the food I left out for you last night," she said.

"We were just so tired, Ma," my mom explained.

I sat down at the table, and Mom slid me a glass of juice. "It looks like a beautiful day," she said, fingering one of the gold hoop earrings she still had on from yesterday.

I nodded.

"Are you going to paddle around the lake by yourself this summer?" Grandma asked me. It was a question she asked me and my cousins every year. Not "How are you?" or "How was your school year?" or "What do you feel like doing most this summer?" Just a question that seemed designed to provoke and, in my case, humiliate.

"We'll see," I said. In other summers, it wouldn't have been easy to make a solo voyage. My cousins were all boys: Max, Rocky, Toad, and Stu — the sons of my dad's brother, Uncle John. They were older than me and much more aggressive. Whenever they were visiting the cabin, I was lucky if I even got a chance to steer the canoe, much less be alone in it. Not that I really minded. Solo canoeing had never been high on my list of summer priorities.

Grandma flipped a pancake on the stove. "How many of these do you eat now?" she asked me.

"Let's say five," I said.

She nodded approvingly. Sometimes I thought she'd be better off with a bear cub than a grandson. Maybe she even wished I was Toad, who'd gotten his nickname as a toddler when he ate a dead housefly off the windowsill and who still ate like an amphibian — all cheeks and tongue.

When she'd finished serving me and Mom, Grandma finally sat down with her own pancake. She didn't show much interest in eating it, though; instead, she wrapped her knobby fingers around her mug and sipped her coffee slowly, like medicine. Grandma had a tough face—tan and leathery from so much time in the sun, and scoured with wrinkles that made her look like she was always frowning. Her white hair was cut short like a boy's, and it lay flat against her head in hard angles. She wore silver glasses—always the same shape and style. They were dull now, but her eyes still glinted behind them when she was in the right mood.

"Did your mother tell you about our newest neighbors?" she asked, gazing slyly at me.

"A new family or something?" I said.

"They have a girl your age!" she said.

"Girls my age are . . ." I hesitated.

Mom listened with obvious interest.

I stuffed the last bite of pancake in my mouth and shrugged. "I don't know."

"Probably starting to look interesting, I'd say," Grandma teased.

I slid off the bench and dumped my dishes in the sink. "I'm going to go down to the dock."

I pushed open the screen door and let it close with a bang, cringing as I heard Mom and Grandma chuckling behind me. Is this what I had to look forward to all summer? Even having my cousins around putting centipedes under my pillow would be better than being the sole object of Mom's and Grandma's attention.

I hopped down the wooden steps of the deck and

followed the worn path that curved around the cabin and down to the lake. The smell of dry pine needles tickled my nose. When I reached the shore, I walked out the length of the dock and stood at its end, taking everything in.

Three Bird Lake was a long oval — more than two miles from end to end and just over a mile across. Small houses dotted the shoreline for most of its perimeter. When my mom was growing up, this had been a summer cabin community with plenty of untouched wooded land. Now most of the neighbors lived here year-round in real houses with grassy lawns. Only Grandma's property was crowded with pines and birches like a genuine northern forest. Lucky for us, she had more than a thousand feet of shoreline and more than a hundred acres of woods. If you stuck to her property, you could still feel like you were someplace wild, even if the other people on the lake owned Jet Skis and plastic flamingos.

The end of the dock was my favorite place on Grandma's property. I spent hours here doing nothing at all. Grandma teased me about it sometimes. "World's best dock-sitter" she sometimes called me. "The neighbors probably think you're a statue, there to scare off the gulls." But I didn't care. I loved the big sky and the big lake rolling out at my feet.

A cool breeze crossed the water. It felt like the great

North was barreling through me with my every breath. Here's what slipped away: schedules, bus rides, the stale smell of the school cafeteria, algebraic equations, Mom and Dad's phone arguments, girl talk, and Grandma's interrogations. Here's what I got in exchange: water sloshing slowly and steadily against the dock like the heartbeat of a great whale. A pair of black-and-white loons swimming into view. Fresh air and a lake that, right then, felt like it was all mine.

I sat down and dropped my feet in the water. It was cold for the middle of June, but I'd get used to it in a few days. Minnows darted at my toes, casting busy black shadows on the sand below.

I heard voices across the water. Grandma's dock was the one place on her property where you were aware of having neighbors. On land, the woods wrapped us in dense cover, but out here, you could see a few nearby docks and the edges of the neighbors' lawns. Now a girl about my age and a boy maybe a couple of years older were standing on the nearest dock, loading a small row-boat with gear. The famous neighbor. Grandma hadn't said anything about a brother, so I figured this was her boyfriend. Maybe that would put an end to Grandma's teasing. Both kids were tall, blond, and tan. Typical Minnesotans. They were probably ace tennis players and competitive Nordic skiers. Not dock-sitters, at least.

I stared across the water at the loons and pretended not to notice the kids. Loons were more interesting anyway. Their heads were glossy and black, with a band of vertical black-and-white stripes around their necks that looked like something they'd stolen from a zebra. Their eyes were red. Across their backs, dozens of small white squares aligned in near-perfect rows.

The two loons drifted closer to me, then abruptly dove underwater. A moment later, I heard the sound of oars clunking against the oarlocks of a boat and looked up to see the two kids rowing into talking range.

"Hey," said the girl. Her long hair was pulled back in a smooth ponytail, and she wore a faded T-shirt from someplace called Camp Watson. "Are you Mrs. Stegner's grandson?"

"Yeah," I said.

The boy was looking at me coolly. I turned my attention to my foot and started picking idly at my big toenail. There were certain boys at my school who turned into total jerks whenever girls were around, and I sensed he was one of them.

"What's the matter? Too much toe jam?" the boy asked.

I pulled my hand away and shrugged. "It's nothing," I mumbled.

"We're going fishing," the girl said. "Want to come?"

The boy's eyes traveled over the inside of the boat, which was already stuffed full with tackle boxes, cushions, and a white plastic pail. "Where's he going to sit — your lap?"

"Very funny, Tyler. There's plenty of room if you slide those worms under your butt," she told him.

Tyler made a face at her.

"That's OK," I said quickly. "I promised my grandmother I'd help her out with some things around the cabin."

"No problem," the girl said. "I'm Alice, by the way. And this is my cousin Tyler."

I nodded. Cousin. So much for my defense against Grandma's teasing.

"You got a name?" Tyler asked when I didn't say anything.

"Uh, yeah. Adam," I said.

He smirked. "Nice."

"See you around!" Alice said, giving Tyler a look.

"Later, Uh-Yeah Adam," said Tyler, whipping his blond hair out of his eyes. He picked up the oars and gave them a strong pull.

I watched them row across the water. A girl on the lake was bad. A girl with an obnoxious cousin was even worse. I couldn't help feeling like my favorite place on earth had just been invaded by enemy forces.

3

LATE IN THE MORNING, I found Mom in the kitchen, her nose buried in the refrigerator. She had been cleaning. The house smelled like Murphy Oil Soap, and the surfaces had an unnaturally shiny glow.

"We need to go to town for food," Mom said, closing the refrigerator door with a hard shove. "There's nothing in here but eggs and a very old ham. I'm not even sure she's gone shopping since Uncle Martin brought her up last month." Uncle Martin was Mom's brother. He lived in the Twin Cities and came up to the cabin for occasional weekend visits.

I glanced out the window at Grandma's station wagon, covered with pine needles. It didn't look like it had been moved in a long time.

"Maybe she doesn't feel like driving anymore," I said.

"Maybe she shouldn't be driving anyway," Mom said quietly, more irritated than concerned. "Come on, let's go to the store so we have something for lunch."

I made a face. "I'd rather stay here."

"I need you to come," my mom said. "I can't keep track of what you like and don't like these days."

"Where's Grandma?" I asked.

"Someplace nearby listening to us, I'm sure," Mom said under her breath. She washed her hands at the sink and dried them on a tattered dish towel.

"Ma?" she called. "Adam and I are going into town for some provisions. Would you like to come?"

We heard a thump from around the corner. Grandma emerged with a dust rag in one hand and a sponge in the other. "Apparently your mother thought this place wasn't spick-and-span enough," she told me with a scowl.

"Mom's a neat freak," I said.

"You've always kept this place neat, Ma," my mom said. "I'm just maintaining tradition."

"The tradition was that there were men around here

20

to do the heavy lifting," Grandma said. "Then we ladies had time for cooking and cleaning."

Mom grimaced, but I couldn't tell if my grandmother was referring to my dad's absence this summer or to the old days, when my grandfather was still alive. From what everyone said, he was a total freak of nature — a big lumberjack of a guy who could chop down a tree, build a shed, fix a leaky pipe, haul out the dock, swim across the lake, and still be back on the deck in time for five o' clock martinis.

"Anyway, we'll stock up on the basics," Mom said, ignoring Grandma's remark. "Are you staying home, then?"

Grandma nodded. We all knew she hated leaving the property. It wasn't so much about driving the Taurus as about seeing herself as a kind of pioneer woman who could exist without modern conveniences. Never mind that she loved an Oreo or two before bedtime.

"Can we get you anything when we're there?" Mom asked.

"You know what I like," Grandma said.

"All right, then," Mom said. She picked up her purse. "We'll be back in time for lunch."

My mom looked strained as she drove out to the main road.

"I knew it," she said. "Something's not right."

"What?" I asked.

"Grandma's different. She's . . . I don't know. I think she's slipping."

I wasn't sure what my mom was talking about. Grandma seemed her usual tough self to me. So what if she forgot what time we were supposed to arrive and hadn't bothered to go grocery shopping? That was just Grandma being stubborn, wasn't it?

"Well, we can help out now," I said.

"Temporarily," Mom said. "And not when she's back in her house in St. Paul."

"Uncle Martin can take care of her there," I pointed out.

"I wouldn't trust Uncle Martin with a pet fish," Mom said.

I gave up. Mom was in one of her arguing moods. I knew she'd just pick apart anything I said.

"And I'm supposed to go to Madison in two weeks for a conference," she went on.

"So go," I said.

"And leave you here?" she asked.

A skinny tree branch whipped in through my open window, and I jerked my head to avoid it. The drive was a challenge under any circumstances, and Mom wasn't driving her best.

"Mom, we'll be totally fine," I said. "Why are you so worked up?"

Just then a deer burst through the trees. Mom braked hard as it bounded across the road. I could see the muscles ripple under its brown hide as it leaped past us and disappeared into the roadside shrubs.

"This place gets wilder and wilder as the rest of the lake gets more and more tame," Mom said.

"Yeah. So?" I asked. I had a strong desire to bolt from the car and run through the bushes like the deer.

"Maybe you could come with me to Madison," she continued as she started driving again.

"Mom, that's stupid," I said. "You just said you don't trust Grandma by herself."

"That doesn't mean I want you looking after her." She shook her head. "You don't see the things I do, Adam."

I was glad for that. More and more, it felt like my mom was one big worry machine. "Well, I still think we can survive a few days," I said finally.

She pursed her lips and drove the rest of the way without saying a word. I stared out the window, relieved to have some silence.

The town of Hubbard Falls looked the same as always. The main street was like something from an

old-fashioned movie set, with a dime store, a movie the-
ater, a candy shop, a soda fountain, and an antique store
filled with old snowshoes, painted duck decoys, and a
real Indian birch-bark canoe. But that part of town lasted
only a few blocks before it intersected a long stretch of
fast-food restaurants and the kinds of chain stores you
could find anywhere in America.

Once we were at the grocery store, Mom shopped
with attitude. She piled the cart high with milk, cheese,
and fresh produce, and stuffed the bottom with a ton of
nonperishables.

"You expecting a snowstorm?" I asked her at one
point.

"Ha-ha."

But it wasn't really a joke. She was like a grocery
shopper with road rage, overfilling the cart in what I
guessed was some kind of statement to Grandma. "This
is food," she seemed to be saying with every box of cereal.
"This is how you stock a kitchen," said the oatmeal, the
sugar, the jam. I finally drifted away to flip through base-
ball magazines. The Cubs were having a rough season,
but I still followed their every game. I didn't rejoin Mom
until she was at the register.

As expected, Grandma looked grim when we brought all
the bags into the cabin.

"I'm not sure where we're going to put all this," Grandma said as Mom started pulling out bags of rice and pasta, cans of soup and tuna.

"I'll take care of it, Ma," my mom said.

Grandma started to empty a bag, then gave a small shrug and returned to the living room, where she had been dusting the mantel.

"All these little nooks and crannies," she complained, poking her dust rag along its edge.

The mantel had an intricate wooden rail around it carved with cutouts of animals. There was a loon, a bear, a beaver, a fish, a squirrel, a wolf, and a deer. As a kid, I'd climb on the brick foundation that wrapped around the fireplace and stretch up to the mantel, running my fingers along the inside of the animal shapes, like tracing stencils in the air.

"I thought you liked that mantel, Grandma," I said now.

"Oh, sure I do," she said. "It's just a pisser to keep the dust out."

She slid the rag into the narrow opening of the loon's beak.

"You can make that my job, if you want," I said.

"You just enjoy the lake," she said. "That's the job for grandsons."

I smiled. Grandma was OK. I was looking forward to

when Mom left for her conference. I pictured Grandma making me pancakes for supper and going to bed so early that I could stay up till midnight without her noticing.

Grandma stopped dusting and furrowed her brow. "Now, what do we have to feed you? Not much, I'm afraid. Do you like ham and biscuits?"

I hesitated, confused. "Grandma, Mom and I just went shopping, remember?" I said. Was it possible she'd forgotten? "We have all sorts of food."

She looked at me for an extra moment and then nodded. "I didn't know you bought lunch food."

I couldn't tell if she was covering for her mistake or if she really meant it.

"Let's go eat," I said quickly, and headed into the kitchen.

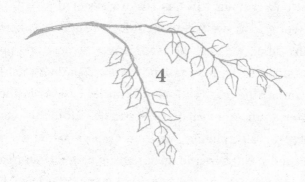

4

FOR A FEW DAYS, Alice and her relatives were a constant, unwelcome presence on the lake, whether or not they were actually in sight. Tyler wasn't the only other kid. There were a couple of boys almost as loud as my cousins, and one little girl who liked to float in a giant inner tube tethered to their dock. I never sat on our own dock when I knew they were outside, choosing instead the hammock under the trees that separated our two properties. I swam only a few times, always listening for the sound of Tyler's mocking voice across the water. I worried, too, that they might discover my grandmother's morning routine — swimming at sunrise before the rest of us were up, with her bathing cap on and her bathing suit off. It seemed normal enough to us after all these years, but that didn't mean she should have spectators. Then one day, the activity around their dock came to an abrupt stop. We learned later that most of the family had gone on a camping trip. Our lake was restored.

For a week, we did all the things we'd always done at the cabin. We took the canoe across the lake and up the Potato River, passing blue herons standing watchful among the reeds and painted turtles basking in the summer sun. Another time we paddled all the way to Hubbard Falls, pulling our canoe ashore at the town park and walking over to the ice-cream parlor. Grandma dug around in the bottom of her purse and came up with enough coins to buy us each an ice-cream cone. Mom didn't mention that she had sixty dollars in her wallet.

On rainy days, we hunkered down in the cabin. Mom had work to do—she was editing manuscripts for a medical journal in Chicago—but Grandma and I stayed busy with cribbage and gin rummy. Other kids would have probably hated being in a cabin without anything but a radio and a telephone to connect them to the outside world. But I liked it. It made me feel farther away from school—like we were trekkers at a remote base camp or polar explorers at a primitive field station.

Grandma spaced out a few times about little things,

like whether she'd made her tea yet and which game we'd decided to play. But it all seemed like pretty minor stuff. Not so different from my mom forgetting my favorite kinds of cookies and breakfast cereal. In a way, it made me feel useful. Like for once I had a job that I could do better than Grandma. I could be Memory Guy.

I spent a whole afternoon lounging on the hammock thinking about what Memory Guy would be like as a superhero. I sketched him with a red cape emblazoned with the letter *M*. I had him tracking down lost sunglasses and car keys and reminding people about their dental appointments. I imagined a major crisis in which vinegar zombies try to take over Earth until Memory Guy remembers the formula for baking soda and neutralizes them in a fury of sticky bubbles.

It occurred to me that Memory Guy could even be the hero of my family. He could help my parents remember the reasons they used to like each other. He could remind them of the promises they'd made to stay together till the bitter end. I tried turning my ideas into a real comic strip, thinking I could mail it to my dad and it would make him chuckle. "Here's one thing you *can* forget," Memory Guy said in one panel. "Those divorce papers!" But something made me stop—maybe it was my pathetic drawing skills, or maybe it was realizing that it probably wouldn't make my dad chuckle at all.

I spent a lot of time down on the dock, of course — sitting, swimming, watching the boats, thinking. There were times I missed the company of my cousins, even if I didn't miss having them boss me around. They had always invented hilarious games on the water — like turning inner tubes into floating basketball hoops or creating a water golf course out of floating life jackets. One time they even set up a bowling alley down the length of the dock; gutter balls became splash balls, and strikes required diving under the water for ten sunken pins. Grandma told my mom that she thought the boys should have been invited to the cabin this year as always, even if my dad wasn't coming. But Mom said it would be too awkward for everyone, especially for her and Uncle John and Aunt Jean. "A lot of things are going to be different from now on, Ma," she'd added. She said it quietly, but of course I heard.

Left on my own so much of the time, I began to think that maybe this *was* the year to start canoeing by myself. I liked imagining the moment when I came up from the dock telling Grandma I'd completed my first circumnavigation. I'd be just like Christopher Columbus standing before the Queen of Spain, minus the long robes and funny tights. But what about all the hard work that came before that? What would it really feel like, I wondered, to be alone on the far end of the lake? Would I be able to control the boat? Would I be strong enough to get it home? What if I tipped over? I eyed Grandma's canoe, a bulky red Old Town sitting overturned on some logs near the shore. It weighed a ton. I wasn't even sure I could get it into the water by myself. So much for Christopher Columbus; in the end, it was easiest just to wait for my mom and grandma to be ready for their next paddle.

At the end of the week, Mom started fretting again about her conference. I could tell she still wasn't comfortable leaving Grandma and me alone. The day before she left, she filled the house with more groceries and kept giving me suggestions for meals I could prepare if Grandma wasn't up to cooking.

Late in the afternoon, I wandered back to my room to get my swim trunks, planning to squeeze in a quick dip before dinner. Standing in front of the dresser, I caught sight of my reflection in the mirror — something that never thrilled me. I lifted up my arm and made a fist. It was totally humiliating: my bicep looked like a small potato. Some guys at school were so ripped, their muscles looked like boulders — boulders that could easily crush a little potato into mush. Maybe I'd start lifting logs this summer and see if it would help me bulk up.

"Do you have enough clean clothes to wear till I'm back?" Mom asked from the other room.

I ignored her.

"Adam?" she called.

I gave up and wandered in. "I'm fine," I said. "I could wear the same shorts and shirt all summer, and it wouldn't matter."

"You'd smell," she said.

"Thanks a lot," I said. "Anyway, I have a bunch of shirts, and you'll only be gone for four days."

She folded her clothes carefully and placed them in her suitcase. "Do you have something to read?"

"There are lots of books here," I said.

"And you've probably read most of them three times already."

"I haven't read *Remembrance of Things Past*. I haven't read *One Hundred Famous Minnesotans*," I said. After all these years, I had managed to memorize most of the titles on Grandma's shelves.

"Yeah, good luck with those," she said. "I'll bring you back something from Madison."

"Cool."

I sat down on the bed, leaned back, and began picking up Mom's little balls of rolled-up socks and tossing them into her open dresser drawer across the room. It was definitely a three-point shot.

"Name two things you liked best about Grandma when you were a kid," I said as I tossed.

"Name what?" she asked. "Oh, Adam, I don't know."

"OK, then two things you didn't like about her," I suggested.

She wrapped the cord of her hair dryer around its handle, then tucked it into the side of her suitcase. She still wasn't answering me.

"You're no fun," I said.

She sighed and combed her fingers through her hair. "OK. Two things I liked most," she said first. "How strong she was — the canoeing and swimming. And how steady."

"And two things you didn't like?" I asked.

"Well, her hairstyle," Mom said. She frowned. "That hasn't changed," she added, speaking quietly even though my grandmother was out on the dock.

"What else?"

Mom paused and looked a little pained. "Well, I didn't always like the way she treated people — me, Martin, even my dad."

I could imagine Grandma being hard on Uncle Martin and my mom — she still was. But my grandfather, too? He was a legend in the family: like Paul Bunyan or something. Grandma boasted about his accomplishments more than anybody else.

"Was she mean?" I asked.

"No, not mean exactly," Mom said. "Just testy."

"Like you?" I asked.

"Not like that at all," she answered quickly, and her face turned red. Just then she became aware of my work with the sock balls. "Hey, what are you doing?" she said, catching the last one in midair. "Those are supposed to go *in* the suitcase!"

"Sorry."

"Listen," she said when she had all the socks back in her bag, "I told the neighbors that you two would be here on your own. Mrs. Jensen is very nice. She said you could come over day or night if you need anything. And they'll take you into town if Ma won't drive, OK?"

"Four days, Mom."

"And you can keep in touch with your dad, of course. Oh, and if you're lonely, Mrs. Jensen said that Alice will be back from camping tomorrow."

"Mom," I said. "Enough about the neighbor girl. How many times do I have to tell you? I like being on my own." I stood up and headed for the door, ready for my swim.

* * *

34

Mom planned to leave very early the next morning, so I said good-bye to her that night. She was sitting at the kitchen table when I went to bed, writing down names and phone numbers and lists of instructions. Sometimes I felt like my mom was only vaguely interested in being a parent until there was some big event or crisis, at which point she became as focused as a general. If you could read affection in someone's to-do lists, my mom's love was deep and very organized.

Early the next morning, I heard the slam of the hatch and sound of the engine starting up, followed by the grinding of tires on dirt and rocks. Eventually the car sounds gave way to a lone loon wailing across the water. *This,* I thought, *this is when freedom begins.* I closed my eyes and fell back asleep.

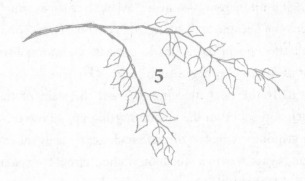

5

AFTER BREAKFAST, Grandma finished washing up, pulled
on her cotton hat, and said, "Come with me."

I followed her out the door and down the steps of
the deck. For a moment, I thought she was planning
to take me for a drive in the Taurus, which would have
been a shocking way to begin our first day on our own
together. But she turned down the path toward the lake,
stopping at the storage area under the cabin to grab a life
jacket and a paddle.

"Are we going canoeing?" I asked.

"Just you," she said, thrusting the paddle and life
jacket into my hands.

I swallowed hard. If she expected me to take off alone across the lake, she was dreaming. A strong breeze was kicking up the water, making it too choppy for easy paddling. Two people could handle it without real difficulty. But it was no place for a beginner to solo.

"Put the canoe in the water," Grandma said.

I was so used to following her orders that I didn't have time to wonder if I was strong enough. I grabbed the far side of the overturned canoe and flipped it over onto the grass. A bigger guy would have carried the whole thing to the lake upside down on his shoulders. But I gripped the deck and dragged the canoe slowly across the mud and into the water.

"Watch the rocks!" Grandma barked. Scratching the bottom of the canoe was considered a major sin in our family. Grandma always shook her head and made an audible *tsk* if we ever passed rocks streaked with the colors of lesser paddlers' boats.

"I won't hit the rocks, Grandma," I said. Amazing. This was my first day of freedom, and my grandmother was already ruining it.

"Get in, get in," she said.

I zipped up the life jacket and stepped into the canoe.

"Now," she said, "are you feeling a little chicken?"

"There's probably a nicer way to say that," I mumbled, but my words were lost in the wind.

37

"It's easy," Grandma said. "You've paddled your whole life. You're strong enough to cart that canoe around. You can do this alone."

"I know I can, Grandma," I lied. I sat down in the stern, then pushed off the side of the dock. I pulled a few strokes on the right side of the canoe, then a few on the left. The bow of the canoe rose high above the water, listing back and forth like a bloodhound that had lost its scent. I wasn't going to win any style points, but at least I was getting somewhere. I pulled past the end of the dock and hit the harder waves. Almost immediately I felt what it was like to lose control. A strong wind caught the bow and shoved it hard to the left. My heart started racing. I dug the paddle in a few times on my left, but I wasn't doing it well. The wind still had me beat by a mile. I listed back toward the shallower water, made a couple of quick strokes on the right side, and managed to turn myself back fully around. Luckily I was out of the harder waves now, too. I slowly brought the canoe back to the dock.

I glanced up at Grandma. She was smiling knowingly. "Is that how your parents taught you?" she asked.

I shrugged. Truth is, I didn't remember anyone teaching me anything — just Max and Rocky and my other cousins showing off their skills and expecting me to watch.

"Let's start at the beginning," she said.

My heart sank. This could go on for hours. Why couldn't Grandma just leave me alone? I had my whole life to learn how to solo canoe.

"First off," she said, "what are you doing in the stern?"

"What?" I asked.

"Your weight back there is what's lifting up the bow. That's why the wind could fling you around like a plastic bag."

Grandma sure had a way with words.

"You sit in the bow seat, facing the stern!"

Of course. I'd seen this done before. No wonder the paddling had felt so hard.

I climbed into the bow seat and faced the middle of the canoe.

"Now," she continued, "you can paddle on both sides like you were doing out there. That'll work easy in a solo canoe. But you might want to pick a side and do your J's and draws, just like you're steering. See which works better for a kid your size."

I ignored the comment about my puny stature and gave it a try.

J strokes were just what they sounded like: you pulled the paddle along the edge of the canoe, then finished with a twist, making a J shape. The twist of the

J turned the paddle into a rudder and kept the bow straight. For a draw stroke, you pulled the paddle toward the canoe before finishing your stroke. That made the canoe turn toward your paddling side. Both of these maneuvers worked easily with a partner, who was usually paddling on the opposite side as you. A little J could even out the power, which was greater in the back than the front. Without anyone paddling in front, though, I didn't know if I could really control the canoe just by executing these moves. Grandma made it sound so easy.

I made a few attempts to paddle as Grandma had instructed, but I preferred paddling on both sides. I wasn't making much better progress, though. Even with my weight more toward the middle, the stern now rose out of the water enough to catch the wind.

"Maybe I should try this again later," I said, returning to the dock. "When it's not so windy."

Grandma didn't reply. She walked back down the dock and picked up a melon-size rock from the shore. I was amazed she was still strong enough to lift a thing like that. Then she made her way back to where I was waiting and squatted down with the rock still in her hands.

"If it's really gusting, you can always kneel in the middle of the canoe," she said. "But this usually does the trick in ordinary wind."

She placed the rock in the stern. The weight was enough to bring the end of the canoe down into a normal position.

"Cool," I said.

She looked me up and down and shook her head. "You're a funny one, Adam," she said. "All these summers on the lake, and the only thing you've ever done by yourself out here is dock-sit. I don't think you've come down even once and fooled around with this stuff on the water."

I looked away, feeling the weight of her judgment. Grandmothers were supposed to shower you with praise, not make you feel like a loser.

I don't know if Grandma realized that she'd hurt my feelings or if she'd just gotten tired of the day's lesson. But she stood back up, brushed off her hands, and turned toward the cabin. "I'll leave you alone to practice," she said, her captain's voice gone.

"OK," I said. "I'll be up in a bit."

What I wanted to do was drag the canoe onto shore and retreat to the hammock. But I knew Grandma would see me there and be more disappointed than ever, so I stayed on the water. I paddled in tentative circles near the shore where the wind wasn't as strong. It felt juvenile and absurd — like riding a pony in a ring. But the idea of heading into open water felt even worse.

I'd been out for about half an hour when I heard voices over in the neighbors' yard. Shouts. Laughter. It sounded as if Alice and her cousins were back from their camping trip. If they came down to the dock, they would see me and my infantile paddling.

Quickly, I steered the canoe to shallow water and heaved it onto shore, more grateful than ever for the sheltering trees.

6

IN THE EVENING, Grandma made me pancakes for supper, just as I had hoped.

"Don't expect these every night," she said.

"It works for me," I said.

"You need protein. Vegetables." Grandma had been a nurse in her younger years, and she still liked to assert her medical knowledge now and then, even if it was sometimes outdated. When I was a kid, she'd caught me stuffing my face with popcorn while I watched TV. "You can't eat that much popcorn," she'd told me then, "or your stomach will explode. I saw it happen once at the hospital. A kid your age."

Her words had terrified me so much I hadn't eaten more than a few kernels at a time for years after. When I was ten, I finally told a friend what she'd said. Just putting it out there in words had been enough for me to realize the ridiculousness of her warning. We'd laughed so hard our stomachs almost did explode. And then we'd gone ahead and eaten two bowls of popcorn and not even felt a cramp.

When Grandma and I finished dinner, she poured herself a cup of coffee and sat back down. She glanced at the clock. "Your mother should have arrived a while ago. I wonder why she hasn't called."

"She stops a lot," I said. I'd almost said "to pee" but Mom was right: that really wasn't something to share with Grandma.

"That so? I don't usually see her slow down for anything," she said crossly.

I shrugged. "Driving's different."

"When are you going to learn to drive?" she asked me.

"I can't even take driver's ed till I'm fifteen," I pointed out.

"You need to know how to drive," Grandma said.

"Grandma, I'm twelve," I said.

Grandma's lips pressed together in a flat line. She looked that way a lot — just kind of annoyed with everything. There were frown lines between her brows that had formed permanent creases. I tried to remember the last time I'd seen her smile.

"You wash up the dishes," she said now. "I'm going to turn in."

"Already?" I asked. This time of year, it could be light for another hour. It hardly seemed like time to go to bed, even for an old lady.

"I like to read awhile," she said. She stood up and set her cup down next to the sink. "You need anything else?"

"Nope," I said.

"Good night, then," she said, making her way back through the living room. "Don't forget to turn off all the lights when you go to bed."

"I won't," I said.

After she left, I stayed sitting, absorbing my new freedom. I'd never been the last one awake at the cabin. I'd never had a chance to feel alone. Maybe I really could stay up till midnight every night that Mom was away.

I got up and filled a bowl with a heap of chocolate ice cream, then went out on the deck to eat it. A motorboat bumped across the lake, and a bird called out a sad two-note song from the pine trees. Grandma would know what kind of bird it was. I'd ask her in the morning.

Thinking of Grandma reminded me that I had dishes to do. I went back inside and filled the yellow tub

45

in the sink with sudsy water, then slid our plates and cups and silverware inside. Grandma didn't have a dishwasher at the cabin, and we'd been using the same tin plates and ceramic mugs my whole life. Probably Mom's whole life, too.

Washing dishes wasn't so bad when there were only two people eating pancakes. Two plates, two cups, two forks, and a batter bowl. Then I was done. I rinsed everything off and placed it on the drying rack. When we had a crowd, someone always dried the dishes by hand, but I couldn't see any reason for that now.

It was still only eight thirty. I tried calling my dad, but he didn't pick up. When the phone rang a few minutes later, I assumed it was him calling back.

"Hi," I said.

"Adam, are you surviving?" It was Mom.

"We're great," I said, trying not to sound disappointed.

"Did you get a good dinner?" she asked.

"Yep," I said, deciding it wouldn't be wise to mention the pancakes.

"Good. Well, I'm here. I made it to town in time for tea with some friends."

She paused, but I didn't say anything.

"Heather and Julie from my old office are here," she

continued, "and a college friend named Anne Marie. She hasn't changed a bit, even though she's gotten married and had three children. Including twins! I don't know how some people stay looking so young."

I stared out the window at the green trees, their colors getting even richer in the fading light.

"So where's Grandma?" Mom asked.

"She turned in," I said.

"Already?"

"She's fine. She had a book to read. It's no big deal."

"What did you two do today?"

"The usual," I said. "I paddled solo for a while." I pictured myself paddling the length of the lake, as steady as a loon, and hoped that's what Mom was picturing, too. "We're fine, Mom."

"Well, good. You'll call if there's any trouble?"

"There won't be," I said.

"OK. Good night, then, sweetie."

"G'night."

After we hung up, I looked at a couple of ancient *National Geographic*s I found on the bookshelf and then walked down to the dock in the fading light. Grandma's dad, my great-grandfather, had chosen his lakefront property so he'd have the best view of the sunset over the lake. It must have been fun being alive when you could still make choices like that — when every lake wasn't overrun with people who had already claimed the best spots.

Standing on the dock, I could see the smallest lines of red and purple at the horizon as the water became gunmetal gray. A loon was swimming off the dock, dipping down below the surface, then popping up as if through an invisible seam. I held my hands together like a ball in front of my mouth and blew through them to make a loud whistle. I could change the pitch by flapping the fingers of my left hand back and forth, creating a pretty great imitation of a loon call — or so I thought. But maybe I was better at playing trumpet than whistling through my hands. The loons didn't respond. They always seemed to save their piercing cries for when we were all in the cabin trying to fall asleep.

I don't know how long I sat there on the dock, my eyes straining to make out familiar shapes even as the light grew dimmer and dimmer. Eventually I wandered back up to the cabin. It couldn't have been midnight yet — probably far from it — but I avoided looking at the kitchen clock so I could at least imagine I'd stayed up that late.

I shut off the cabin lights and felt my way back to the bedrooms. Cabin dark was the purest darkness I knew, and I hadn't yet gotten used to walking blind. The door of my room was shut, and I felt for the knob. As I turned and pushed the door open, I heard the sound of something light and papery slipping to the ground. I closed the door and switched on my bedside lamp. There on the floor was a folded-up piece of paper. What was this — a note? Did Grandma think I needed a reminder to wash the dishes or turn out the lights?

I unfolded the paper, prepared to take a glance and toss it in the trash. But the greeting caught my eye.

My love,
I buzz around the cabin all day thinking of you.
Don't forget to pick up crackers tomorrow. Mole's
in the meadow! Beaver's in the lodge!
Viola

I read the note three times. Viola was my grandma's name, and I recognized her handwriting, but what did she mean? I wasn't going anywhere where I could get crackers, and she'd never called me her "love" before. Clearly the note was for somebody else. My mom, maybe? But why would she need crackers at her conference? Besides, Grandma wouldn't call Mom her "love," either, and she would have signed it "Ma." So who was this note for? And why had she stuck it in my door?

I folded up the paper again and put it on my bedside

stand. As I brushed my teeth in the bathroom, I puzzled over the mystery. Maybe it was left over from the time when my grandfather was still alive, and it had been stashed away in the bookcase across from my room. When I'd pulled out the *National Geographic*s, I'd probably knocked the note loose. Grandma must have seen the folded paper on the floor, assumed it was mine, and stuck it in my doorway. It was nice of her, actually, not to invade my privacy by reading it or putting it in my room.

I rinsed out my mouth, picked up the note, and slid it back between a couple of books.

Mystery solved.

7

IN THE MORNING, there was a pattering sound on the leaves outside my window, and a steady plink on the metal gutters. Rain. I didn't mind — the cabin felt like a rain forest tree house in a good shower, especially when the rain started in the morning and lasted all day. Grandma had already switched on some lamps in the living room and the kitchen, and was setting my pancakes on a plate.

"I thought you'd never wake up," she said. "How late did you stay up last night?"

"Not very late," I said, scratching my head.

"I see you didn't have time to dry the dishes." She scowled.

I frowned. "I—"

"Or clean the griddle," she continued.

She had me there. "Sorry, Grandma. I spaced out about the griddle."

"You what?"

"I forgot."

She gave a little scornful exhale through her nose, like a dog fighting a sneeze.

"Today's a rain day. Might last all week, according to the radio. You got a project or something?"

I shrugged. "I don't mind cabin days," I said. "I can read and stuff."

After breakfast Grandma turned on her old stereo and played a recording of a horn concerto. I offered to do the morning dishes to make up for my lapses the night before. Then I pulled a book off the shelf—a guide to reptiles and amphibians—and settled into a comfortable spot by the window to read about venomous snakes.

Sitting in one place like that, I became aware for the first time of how much Grandma wandered around. She'd go to her bedroom. Reappear for a few minutes. Duck back in. Walk back out and go to the kitchen. Open a drawer, poke through. Sigh. Go back to her room. It didn't really seem like she'd lost something— more like she was keeping herself busy with puttering.

Eventually, though, she settled down on the couch and read her own book.

In the afternoon, we were playing crazy eights at the kitchen table when a car appeared on the drive and pulled in beside Grandma's station wagon.

"Now, who could that be?" Grandma asked, sounding flustered.

"Maybe it's a pizza guy!" I said hopefully.

Grandma frowned at me. We opened the door and peered out. The car doors swung open, and a tall woman emerged on one side and Alice on the other.

Ugh.

"Hello, hello!" the woman called, obviously Alice's mother.

Alice gave me a slight nod.

Grandma and I stared, like two dumb chickens watching the farmer clamber into their henhouse. We weren't used to visitors.

"We thought you might be feeling a little stranded in all this rain," Alice's mom said, popping open her trunk and pulling out a couple of bags of groceries.

She walked up to the house and gave me a smile. "You must be Adam," she said. "I'm Mrs. Jensen, Alice's mom. Alice tells me you two have already met."

I nodded uncomfortably.

Alice smiled at Grandma. "Hi, Mrs. Stegner," she said.

"Hello, dear," said Grandma, finding her manners quicker than I'd found mine. "Come on in and out of this rain!"

Alice and her mom followed Grandma into the cabin, and I came up slowly behind them. Mrs. Jensen set the groceries on the kitchen table and held her arms up in amazement. She was wearing a floral skirt and a sleeveless shirt, and her arms had soft, droopy skin. "What a beautiful place!" she exclaimed. "Just look at those windows!"

Grandma smiled proudly.

"You can see the lake from up here?" Mrs. Jensen asked.

"It's there," Grandma said. "Behind the rain."

Mrs. Jensen laughed, a great big laugh that seemed to emanate from deep inside her. I had this image of her as a giant pump with her arm for a handle and the laughter like water that gushed when you pumped it.

"Have you been coming up here for long, Adam?" Mrs. Jensen asked me.

I nodded. "Ever since my grandma was a kid."

Alice and her mother burst into laughter. "Wow. You must be old!" Alice exclaimed.

I felt myself blush and stammered, "I — I mean, the

cabin has been here ever since my grandma was a kid. So I've been coming my whole life."

"We knew what you meant," Mrs. Jensen said kindly.

"I was in high school," Grandma said, sounding vaguely annoyed. "I was hardly a kid."

Mrs. Jensen wandered farther into the cabin, examining the details around the windows and the cushioned benches beneath them. "This woodwork is gorgeous! And I love the way the porch rail is finished," she said, pointing out the window. Instead of being flat, the top rail of the porch had been made with a sawtooth edge — small triangles lined in a row.

"It's supposed to make you think of the waves on the lake," I explained.

"And what's this flag?" she asked, turning her attention to the fireplace wall.

"That's our Three Bird Lake banner," I said.

"Golly!" said Mrs. Jensen. "Someone sure knew how to sew!"

"That was my mother's work," Grandma said. "My father designed it."

"They should sell replicas of it in town," said Mrs. Jensen. "I bet they'd sell like hotcakes."

My grandmother sniffed. I could tell she had no interest in anyone else owning a bit of our family's creativity. And, frankly, I didn't either.

"I like this part," Alice said as she walked toward the mantel. "Look at all the animals!" I noticed her finger went immediately to trace the inner curves, just like mine always had.

"Did your father make this, too?" Alice asked Grandma.

"Wasn't it the builder or something, Grandma?" I said.

"The builder's son," she said, correcting me. "My father designed almost everything in the cabin, right down to the benches and tables, and he helped the builder make it all, too. But neither one of them had an eye for that kind of detail work."

"Well, it's all extraordinary," Mrs. Jensen said with a sigh. "A gem of a cabin. Folks around here wonder about this place. It's hard to see, even from the water. I'm sure no one has any idea what a treasure it is."

Grandma nodded proudly. "Those who should appreciate it do," she said simply.

"So, Adam," Mrs. Jensen said, turning to me. "What do you do to keep yourself busy up here?"

I shrugged. "The usual stuff. Swim. Canoe. Goof around outside. Today we've just been hanging out in the cabin."

She gave me a concerned maternal look. "You should come over to our place!" she said.

I stole a glance at Alice, who looked uneasy. I should have guessed. Girls had that way of smiling sweetly in front of other people but showing their claws when grown-ups turned their heads.

"You have a lot of guests," I said, trying to find a polite way out.

"Not anymore," Mrs. Jensen said. "It's back to Alice, her dad, and me. We have games. TV. Ping-Pong. Wireless. What else are you supposed to do in all this rain?"

I nodded uncomfortably. Alice stared out the window.

"So visit us!" she said. "It's either that or — what? Read the dictionary?" She burst out laughing at her own joke.

"Thanks. I'll think about it," I finally mumbled.

There was an uncomfortable silence. I think it was Grandma's moment to invite Alice and her mom to stay for a cup of tea or something. But Grandma seemed to have reached the limits of her sociability.

"Well, it was nice of you to stop by," she said. "You probably want to get back and put those groceries away."

Luckily, Mrs. Jensen didn't seem to take offense. "Oh, these are for you! Your daughter mentioned that you'd be without a driver while she was away, so Alice and I thought we'd pick you up a few things while we were out."

"You really shouldn't have," Grandma said. I eyed her nervously, wondering if she was going to get grumpy with Mrs. Jensen the way she did with Mom.

"Oh, it was our pleasure!" Mrs. Jensen said. She turned to me. "There's ice cream in one of those bags. You'll want to put that in the freezer right away."

"We got chocolate chocolate chip," Alice said to me. "Hope that works for you."

Chocolate chocolate chip was one of my favorites, but I didn't feel like mentioning that to Alice.

"Sure," I said.

"You really shouldn't be worrying about us," Grandma said. "Bobbie only left yesterday. And she'll be home the day after tomorrow!"

"Well, it's hard to keep the milk fresh," said Mrs. Jensen. "Now, call if you need anything else." She turned to me. "And I meant that about coming over. Alice gets lonely these days, too!"

Alice didn't look like the kind of girl who ever got lonely. And, in fact, I caught her rolling her eyes again.

"Good-bye now," Mrs. Jensen called. "You two take care!"

"Bye," Alice said.

We watched them get back into their car, turn

around, and disappear down the drive. Then we stayed staring for a few moments longer . . . still a couple of dumb chickens, I guess, trying to figure out what had just happened. We headed back into the cabin, which felt strangely empty now without Mrs. Jensen's big laughter filling up every corner.

8

boredom: (noun) the state of being weary and restless through lack of interest. Synonyms: blahs, doldrums, ennui, listlessness, tedium.

blahs: a general feeling of discomfort or dissatisfaction.

doldrums: a period of inactivity or state of stagnation.

ennui: listlessness and dissatisfaction arising from lack of interest.

listlessness: lacking energy or disinclined to exert effort.

tedium: the quality or state of being tedious. *See* boredom.

I closed the dictionary. After four more days of rain, I was getting to know boredom so well, I hardly needed the dictionary: I could have written a whole encyclopedia.

At home, there'd been an itchy restless kind of boredom, like when Mom delivered a monologue about the "fascinating" trip her colleague had taken to a French monastery.

At school, there'd been the zoned-out kind of boredom of listening to a bad teacher drone on for an hour, making my brain sink into sleep mode like an idle computer.

On the road, there'd been the kind of suffocating boredom that comes from being inside a car with the windows rolled up and nothing to look at but the dust on the dashboard and the yellow and white lines on the pavement.

But here at the cabin, there was a different kind of boredom altogether — a monotony that made time slow down in a crazy way. I didn't feel itchy or tired or suffocated. I just felt emptied out. Was this how the pioneers felt living day after day with nothing but the trees for company? Except they had the drama of survival, and I didn't even have that, what with a snug cabin, electricity, and a stocked fridge.

Across the room, Grandma had her head tilted back on the sofa cushion and was taking her afternoon siesta.

Mom was cleaning out the storage area under the cabin. She'd come home late Thursday night, and now we were back to healthy dinners and not-so-healthy bickering. Maybe the bickering was why she'd decided to clean the storage area. It was as far away as someone could get from the main part of the cabin without having to be out in the rain.

After slipping the dictionary back onto the bookshelf, I spent a little while staring at my toes and trying to imagine how much farther they were away from my head than they used to be. I got out an old marker and drew fake freckles on my arm. I leaned my head back against the chair and stared at the Three Bird Lake banner, then closed my eyes to see if I could remember the placement of each beak, every feather. I opened my eyes and checked my accuracy. Closed them and tried again. Finally I stood up. I had to get out of here. So what if it was raining? A little rain couldn't be worse than this.

I went outside and walked to the end of the dock. The lake was dark and gray like the sky above. Raindrops stippled the surface of the water, but there wasn't much of a wind.

I walked up to the storage area, where I could hear my mom shoving boxes around on the concrete floor. "Want to go for a paddle?" I called.

"What's that?" she asked, popping up from behind Uncle Martin's old catamaran. Her hair was pulled back in a bandanna, and she wore work gloves. She was taking this cleaning job very seriously.

"Want to go for a paddle?" I asked again.

"Oh, I'm sorry, Adam, but I'm really in the middle of things here. And I vowed I'd get all the deep cleaning done this week so I can get back to my editing."

"I guess I'll go out on my own, then," I told her, hoping she'd feel sorry for me and change her mind.

But all she said was "Good for you."

I hesitated, then picked up a life jacket and a paddle from the hooks on the wall.

Down at the dock, I hauled the canoe into the water and climbed inside, sitting backward in the bow seat as Grandma had taught me to do. One quick push off the dock, and I was on my way.

The rain wasn't so bad even on the lake. It felt more like a tickly kind of mist than a real shower. I started paddling along the edge of Grandma's property, staying close to the shoreline. The bluff rose so steeply here that all I could see on my right was a wall of green — no cabin, no people. It felt strangely wild, as if I'd entered a different world, where anything was possible. Would I come upon a nesting loon? Would a moose suddenly rise up out of the shrubs, water dripping from its antlers?

I paddled quietly and looked hard. But all I saw were a lot of wet shrubs without so much as a grasshopper in sight. Maybe the animals, too, had decided to make it a cabin day.

Eventually Grandma's woods gave way to the grounds of the neighboring church camp. I had to turn away from the shoreline and head out into open water to avoid the camp swimming area, bounded off by ropes. None of the campers were out now, but I heard the faint sound of singing coming from one of the buildings. I stopped paddling and floated offshore. I was the only person on the water. I was an explorer. I was a spy.

I suppose if I'd been really brave, I would have taken off for the marsh on the other side of the lake. But in a way it was more fun to linger on the edge of civilization. Besides, when I turned the canoe back in the direction of Grandma's cabin, I discovered that the rain was blowing straight into my face. I had to paddle hard, pausing now and then to wipe the water out of my eyes.

As I rounded the last bend in the shoreline, I saw a figure sitting on the edge of the Jensens' dock. I dipped my paddle gently into the water, hoping to be silent and blend in with the curtain of mist. But it was Alice, and she had no trouble spotting me. When I turned the canoe in for a landing, she stood up and waved, beckoning me over. Reluctantly, I shifted course and paddled over to her dock. At least I'd had some time to practice my skills before paddling solo in front of her.

"Hi," she said. Her hair was loose, and she was wearing a T-shirt, cutoffs, and faded Converse sneakers. "You're soaked!"

I shrugged. "It's raining."

She laughed, a junior version of her mother's big laugh. She thought I was making a deadpan joke. I tried to look like someone who said funny, deadpan things.

She eyed the canoe. "Can I get in?" she asked.

"Um, OK," I said uncomfortably. "You don't mind getting wet?"

"I'm not exactly staying dry sitting here!" Alice said, laughing again.

"Oh, right," I said. "You need a paddle, though. And a life jacket."

"How very Boy Scouty of you," she responded. "Let me go check our storage box."

She started to turn away, but I stopped her.

"Um, you know what?" I said. "I was actually just about to go in. I mean, I'm pretty soaked, like you said . . ."

"Oh, OK," she said. "Sure thing."

It was a relief to be off the hook. Or sort of, anyway. Alice looked at me like she was sizing me up, girl style. Those X-ray eyes.

"Would you be interested in trying again tomorrow, or not so much?" she ventured.

"Sure," I said, out of excuses.

"If you bring an extra paddle, I'll be sure to have my life jacket on," she said. "Scout's honor," she added, holding up her hand in a mock pledge.

I smiled. "Okeydoke," I said, sounding just like my mom. But Alice let it go.

"We have this bell," she said, pointing to an old black bell hanging on the end of the dock. "Just ring!"

I nodded and paddled home. I really was soaked, and I felt cold, shivery, and strangely unsettled now.

But I didn't feel bored. Definitely not bored.

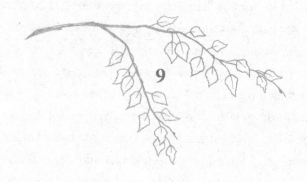

9

"I'M GOING IN to take a shower," I called to my mom as I returned the life jacket and paddle to the storage area.

She was standing over my grandfather's old work-bench, dropping nails and screws into rusty coffee cans. "How was your paddle?" she asked, not bothering to look up.

"Good," I said.

"See anything interesting out there?"

"Nope," I said, turning away. My ears had a habit of turning red when I was embarrassed, and I didn't want to take a chance that Mom would see them now.

"I'm going to take a break in a minute," she said. "I need to go to town for more cleaning supplies. Want me to wait for you?"

"Nah, you go ahead," I said.

I went inside and took a long, hot shower. Afterward I stood in front of the mirror over my dresser. I combed my wet hair, then checked out my arm muscles again. So far the paddling hadn't had any visible effect; I was still the proud owner of a pair of egg-size muscles. I frowned and pulled on a clean T-shirt. It was then that I noticed something new tucked into the corner of the mirror. Below the postcard and the picture of me from kindergarten was a folded-up piece of paper, like the note that had fallen off the bookcase. I tugged it out and opened it up. Sure enough, it was a note from Grandma. But not the same one as before.

I sat on my bed and read it through.

My love,
Have you been hearing the loons out on the lake?
One calls and then the other answers, like two
halves of one heart, yearning to be whole again.
Isn't that just how it feels?
Missing you loonily,
Viola

I reread the note, then looked up at the mirror. Could it have been there all along, and I just hadn't noticed it till now? Doubtful but not impossible. But why would Grandma store old personal notes in such a public place? She was usually much more private than that.

Or maybe the note wasn't old. The paper was crisp and white, and the handwriting was Grandma's shaky old-lady cursive. This wasn't an old note to my grandfather. It was a *new* note to him. And he'd been dead for twenty years!

I got up and paced around the room as the truth of the situation hit me. Grandma was slipping. Really, really slipping. Here Mom thought she was just getting forgetful, when she was actually losing her mind. Why else would she be writing love letters to my dead grandfather? Did she think he could read her notes from beyond the grave? Did she think he could really still hear the loons? The whole thing was way too weird.

I folded up the note and went to find Mom, but the car was gone. She must have still been in town. Grandma was sitting up on the living-room couch, done with her nap and looking out the window with a pair of binoculars.

"You ever notice how a nuthatch moves down a tree trunk?" Grandma asked.

"I don't know," I said, checking to see if I could spot Mom's car approaching through the trees. No luck.

Grandma still had her binoculars trained on one spot. "Imagine hopping down a vertical surface head-first. And we humans think we're so great!"

I ignored her. What I really wanted to do was to go outside and get as far away from Grandma as possible till Mom showed up, but I didn't feel like getting wet again. Instead, I rummaged in the pantry and dug out some pretzels, then sat at the table and munched on them while I looked at a week-old newspaper.

"What are you eating there?" Grandma asked. It felt like she'd turned to train her binoculars on me, but when I looked up, she had her head back on the seat cushion with her eyes closed.

"Nothing, Grandma. Just leave me alone, OK?" I said.

"Humph," she said. She put her hands down on the arms of the chair and pushed herself into a standing position. "Fine way to talk. And you call yourself a gentleman," she muttered, standing up and retreating to her bedroom.

I shuddered, not entirely sure she knew whom she was talking to.

* * *

Not long after, my mom's car pulled into the driveway. I was waiting for her when she came through the doorway with her arms full of groceries.

"Mom," I said, "we have to talk."

"Fine, but could you grab some bags from the car first?" she asked. "The back is still open, and those bags are going to get soaked."

I grudgingly jogged out to the car and yanked two bags from the back. By the time I'd brought them to the kitchen, Mom was already heading out for more.

"Mom," I said.

"Look at the rain, Adam!" she said.

This time I heard her slam the hatch before she came inside. I held open the door, and she dropped the final two bags on the counter and wiped off her brow.

"The amount of food you two eat could feed a small army," Grandma said, coming into the kitchen and peering into the bags.

Mom grimaced and shook out her raincoat. "What was it you needed to tell me, Adam?" she asked.

With Grandma hovering over us, I'd lost my chance. "Never mind," I said.

"Well, let's get these things put away," Mom said. "I'd like to start dinner. We're having a surprise guest!"

Grandma and I looked up in alarm. Mom laughed. "Don't look so scared, you two! It's just Dottie Lewis! I ran into her at the market. She misses you, Ma. Said she hasn't seen you yet this summer."

Dottie was one of Grandma's oldest friends on the lake, though they never seemed to spend much time together anymore.

Grandma peered at the clock. "Well, I wish you'd given me a little more warning. I would have baked something special."

"It was just a spontaneous thing," Mom said. "But I bought some fresh berries, and there's still plenty of time to make a pie."

Grandma perked up a little at that. She strode to the pantry and retrieved an apron.

"It'll take me a few more minutes to get the table cleared off," Mom told her. "Have a seat."

Grandma sat down, awaiting her supplies. Or her instructions. It was hard to tell which when Mom was involved. Either way, I could tell there wasn't room for me in all this. I grabbed the newspaper and another handful of pretzels and went back to my room.

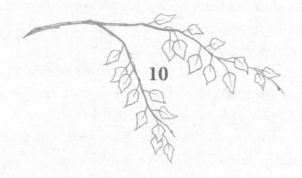

10

DOTTIE LEWIS BROUGHT OUT the best in my grandmother. From the moment she stepped into the cabin, Grandma's expression changed. Her face lifted up in a way that erased her scowl and made her look friendlier. She had changed into a nicer tucked-in blouse and put on some makeup. I'd always thought makeup was a little freaky. But at her age, it had its advantages.

Dottie was the same age as my grandmother, but she acted a decade younger. She had her long hair pulled back in a bun and wore bright lipstick that matched the big red beads on her necklace.

"Guess what!" she told my grandmother. "I've gotten into clay!"

"Clay?" Grandma asked. "In the garden?"

"No, Viola!" Dottie laughed. "I'm talking pottery. Ceramics. You should see me, Adam — I'm like an old witch sitting in front of that potter's wheel. I put my hands on the wet clay and — abracadabra! — I'm making the wildest creations!"

"That's remarkable, Dottie," my mother said. She circuited the table to make sure everyone was taking salad. I nodded in agreement.

"You'll have to show me your work sometime," Grandma said with careful bites of her lettuce.

"I will!" Dottie said enthusiastically. "I'll take you over to the studio sometime."

"Did you really just start making pottery, like, this year?" I asked. I couldn't imagine my grandmother starting something new at this age.

She nodded. "The last time I messed around with clay at all was almost seventy years ago. And you were there, Viola!" she said with a wink.

"Not at scout camp?" my grandmother asked.

Dottie nodded. "I made something truly awful. I think it was a miniature wishing well."

"I made a grizzly bear," my grandmother said, surprising us all with her sudden recollection. "I tried to

74

make it hulking and terrifying — a real predator. But when I showed it to my father, he thought it was our dog, Ollie."

Dottie burst out laughing. "Ollie? That tiny dachshund?"

Grandma nodded. "So much for my sculpting talent!" she exclaimed.

Dottie's laugh was so infectious that the two of them started laughing like kids, and my mom and I couldn't help but join in. Grandma dabbed at her eyes with her napkin. "Now you know why I've never touched a piece of clay again."

"Oh, well, you should try," Dottie said. "You might be surprised."

"Besides," Mom said, "realism's gone out of fashion. You might find you have quite a knack."

They talked and laughed like that straight through dessert and coffee, reminiscing about the hilarious skits they had performed, the pranks they had played, the crazy eagle hats they had made for one Fourth of July parade.

Finally Dottie said she should leave before it got any darker outside, or she'd end up running into one of the trees on our drive. "That little road of yours seems longer every time I come out here," she told my grandmother. "You can't call it a driveway."

"It's not," Grandma said proudly. "It's what separates me from all that . . . change."

Dottie nodded and looked around the room. "It's true. You stay here for a while, you almost start to feel like you've traveled back in time. Except for you, young man," she said, reaching up and rubbing the top of my head. "You're our connection to the younger generation. And they're running the world now, you know!" she told Grandma.

Grandma clucked her tongue. "Don't encourage it. They're already too full of entitlement," she said.

"I like to encourage it," Dottie told me conspiratorially. "Kids like you give me hope!"

After Dottie left, Grandma went straight to bed, and Mom and I did the dishes.

"Ma seemed so good tonight!" my mom exclaimed. "Don't you think?"

I nodded. I knew this was my chance to tell her about Grandma's notes, but somehow I couldn't bring myself to say anything. All evening Grandma had acted so normal again. And Mom seemed happier than she'd been in ages. Why should I stir up trouble?

"They sure were goofy back in the old days," I said. "They really made hats with eagles on them?"

"I think they had a lot of fun," Mom said. She handed

me a soapy plate. "It was a lot of old-lady talk, though, Adam. Are you sure *you're* having enough fun?"

"I'm fine," I told her. Suddenly I remembered my plans with Alice. Between finding the note and having Dottie over for dinner, I'd forgotten all about my promise to go paddling with her tomorrow.

As I dried the last dish, I found myself wondering what it would be like to paddle with a girl. Would she be nice? Would she boss me around? And what were we ever going to find to talk about for an entire canoe trip?

I said good night to my mom and headed back to my room, full of dread.

11

WAKING UP AT THE CABIN was usually the complete opposite of a school day, when you'd be scrambling to get to the bus on time or worrying about a test. You didn't scramble at the cabin. You just opened your eyes slowly, breathed in the forest air, sniffed for breakfast, and listened to the stirrings of whoever was already up. Then you either rolled out of bed or just stayed, burrowing under the blankets and enjoying the warmth a little longer. There was no schedule, no hurry, no dread.

But not this morning. From the moment I woke up, I felt weighed down by the day's plans, which now seemed like more than I could handle. Why had I let Alice ruin my cabin peace? And wasn't there some way to get out of this? I peered out the window, half hoping that the rain had gotten worse in the night. But the clouds were gone. It looked like it was going to be a beautiful day.

Darn.

After I ate my pancakes, I offered to do the dishes.

"Nonsense," Grandma said, taking my syrupy plate from me. "Get outside and start enjoying that sun before it decides to go AWOL on us again."

I found Mom back in her room with her pile of manuscripts.

"I'm going paddling," I told her.

"OK," she said, not looking up.

I hesitated. Wasn't there something she was going to tell me to do instead? Some reason I couldn't go? "I may be gone awhile," I said.

"That's fine."

Slowly, I made my way outside. The wooden slats of the deck were still damp from all the rain, but they weren't going to stay that way for long. The sky was piercingly blue, and a light dry wind was blowing across the water.

I got two paddles and a life jacket from the shed and took them down to the water's edge. I wanted to feel totally normal, but in fact I was jumpy. Lugging the canoe across the wet ground, I slipped and dropped it hard on my foot. I was glad no one was there to see me, but I doubted it was going to be my last screw-up of the day.

I set the canoe in the water and paddled over toward Alice's dock. By the time I pulled alongside it, she was striding down the lawn beside a man I guessed was her father. He looked jolly. She looked miserable. Was there a chance he'd told her she couldn't go?

"Good morning, Adam!" the man said with a friendly smile. "I'm Dan Jensen." He put out his right hand to shake mine, but I was using it to hold on to the dock. When I let go, the boat drifted just enough that I couldn't reach him. I grabbed for the paddle and drew closer again, and this time he just slapped me on the shoulder. "Never mind about the handshake. Good to meet you."

I nodded, speechless as usual. Alice was pulling on her life jacket, so I guessed the trip was still on.

"Do you have everything you need?" I asked her. I climbed down the length of the canoe and took my place in the stern.

"Whoa, there," said Mr. Jensen. "A boy's got to go through a little basic interrogation before he makes off with my daughter. Especially on the high seas."

I felt my face go red. I was getting a sense of why Alice looked miserable.

"Do you know what you're doing in this craft?"

"Yeah," I said dumbly. I hoped he hadn't seen me out there learning to solo paddle the first time.

"Do you know how to swim?" he asked.

"Sure," I said.

"How well do you know the lake?"

Alice spoke up. "I told you, Dad. He's been coming to the lake since he was a kid."

"Well, he's not much more than a kid now!" Mr. Jensen laughed. "And you're still a baby!"

Alice rolled her eyes. "We're going, Dad," she said, and climbed into the front of the canoe. She reached back for the second paddle, and I passed it up to her.

"Wait! Wait!" a high, quavering voice called out. We looked up to see Mrs. Jensen trotting down the path from the house with a cloth grocery bag in her arms. She was breathless when she reached us. "I packed you kids a little picnic. I thought you might get hungry out there."

"Thanks, Mom," Alice said grudgingly.

"Yeah, thanks, Mrs. Jensen," I said.

Mr. Jensen stowed the bag between me and Alice — underneath the thwart, the wooden bar that spanned the canoe in front of my seat. "There," he said. "I think you're set. Do you have your cell phone?" he asked Alice.

Alice patted the pocket of her shorts. "Right here. See you guys later."

Taking her cue, I shoved off the dock.

"Good-bye! Have fun! Be safe!" her parents called as we made our way across the water.

I chose the shoreline route to start us off so we'd be out of their sight as quickly as possible. Unfortunately this meant passing my cabin again, which put me at risk of a sighting and an interrogation from Mom and Grandma when I got back. But if they had their noses pressed up to the windows as we paddled past, I couldn't tell.

Neither of us said anything till we had rounded the bend, away from the docks and our families. Then Alice sighed and twisted around to face me. "Sorry," she said. "My parents can be so embarrassing."

"No problem," I said. It had hardly been worse than when she'd met my Grandma.

"I wonder if you can justifiably complain that your parents love you too much," she mused.

A pair of blue damselflies whirred past my shoulder and came to rest on top of Alice's paddle. She held the paddle aloft and watched them linger there. When they flew off, she continued paddling.

"Do you think?" she asked.

"What?" I asked dumbly.

"That parents can actually love you too much?"

I hesitated. It wasn't something that I had ever thought about before. My brain felt blank, and it occurred to me that Alice was moments away from realizing that I was a complete dud.

"I mean, do *your* parents love you too much?" she asked. "In that squeezy, suffocating, we'll-have-a-fit-if-you-break-a-fingernail kind of way?"

"I don't know," I said. "I don't think so." My parents didn't seem to love me too much or too little. They were just . . . parents.

"You're lucky, then," Alice said. She gave a few especially strong strokes of her paddle, and we sped across the water. "God, I wish I had a brother or sister."

I didn't say anything.

"Do you have any siblings?" she asked.

"No," I said.

"Where's your dad?"

"Back in Chicago."

She looked over her shoulder. "You don't talk much, do you?"

I shrugged uncomfortably. Alice was turning out to be even chattier than my mom.

"Where are we headed, anyway?" she asked me cheerfully, as if she couldn't wait to get started on a big adventure.

What I wanted to say was "How about home?" But I wasn't brave enough to say that. Instead, I mumbled, "Wherever you want."

She thought for a moment. "Can we paddle up the Potato River?" she asked. "I've heard it's amazing. And I wouldn't mind being away from my parents all day."

The Potato River? Gone all day?

"OK," I said reluctantly. This was going to be the longest day of my life.

I pulled the paddle into a draw stroke and got us turned back toward the middle of the lake. The wind felt stronger in this direction. By the time we were in the middle of the lake, the waves were sloshing against the side of the canoe, and we had to paddle with effort. It was exciting but daunting, too. I wondered if Alice and I were experienced enough to be out here on our own after all.

Once we reached the other side of the lake, the wind and waves quieted down and we could relax again. We slowly approached the marshy entrance to the river, where cattails grew in dense clumps, and the spaces between were covered with a mat of lily pads.

"Where do we go from here?" Alice asked. A canoe didn't need much water to get through, but it was still important to choose the right route. Otherwise you'd end up stuck on mud or running into a wall of reeds.

"My mom and grandma and I went this way last time." I pointed out a channel to the right, and we steered ourselves down it. The canoe made a soft swishing noise as we skimmed over the lily pads.

We pushed off the lake bottom with our paddles whenever we got stuck, and then the river opened up and the paddling grew easier again. At first there were a few houses with lawns that ran right to shore, and it almost felt like we were trespassing on private property. But soon we reached the wilder stretches of the river and settled into a smooth rhythm, even as we were working against the light current.

"My parents never do this," Alice said. "They're not as wildernessy as your family."

"I thought you went camping last week," I said.

Alice laughed. "My aunt and uncle took us up north to an RV park. We had a big-screen TV!"

"Oh," I said.

"Definitely not wildernessy," she said, shaking her head.

After about an hour of paddling and, thankfully, not much conversation, we passed a small island. On its banks were marks in the mud where other people had pulled their canoes ashore.

"Want to stop here?" Alice asked.

"Sure," I said. I steered in with a hard stroke,

sending the front of the canoe sliding onto the mud. Alice stepped into the water, sneakers and all, and pulled the canoe forward. Her parents may not have been wildernessy, as Alice put it, but somewhere along the line she had learned good canoeing skills.

We stowed our paddles and took off our life jackets. Alice was wearing a green tank top that showed off her strong, lean arms. I had a sneaking suspicion that her biceps might even have been bigger than mine, but I refused to look closely enough to find out.

We sat down on a rock. Alice peered into the bag her mother had given us.

"OK," she said. "Forget what I said. I'm glad my parents love me too much."

"Yeah?" I said.

"We've got sandwiches," she said, pulling out four squares crisply wrapped in wax paper. "We've got cold drinks," she continued, pulling out two water bottles glistening with condensation. "Chips, fruit, healthy vegetable matter. And best of all," she said, reaching in with a smile, "Grandma Hattie's mint chocolate-chip cookies!"

She offered me a sandwich, which I unwrapped and started eating.

"It's a funny thing about those cookies. Grandma Hattie isn't my grandma at all. She's my friend Yolanda's grandmother. But the cookies are so good, I might adopt Grandma Hattie."

I wasn't sure why Alice was telling me any of this, but at least it filled the space. I kept eating.

"God, I miss Yolanda," she went on. "It's so quiet up here! Don't you think?"

I shrugged. "Sort of."

"Doesn't it get weird with just you and the ladies?" she asked.

I thought about how much weirder it was than Alice would ever know. A mother who spent so much time working and worrying she hardly seemed to notice she was on a beautiful lake. A grandmother writing notes to a dead man. But I shook my head. "Not really."

"Really? You don't need friends?"

She probably hadn't meant to be mean, but her question stung. I put down my sandwich. "I didn't say that," I said. "I just don't need to be surrounded by a bunch of popular kids to have fun."

"Who said anything about popular kids?" Alice asked.

I shrugged.

"You think I'm popular?" she asked. She let out one of her big guffaws. "I would love for Tiffany Ellis to hear you say that. She thinks I'm a freak of nature!"

I looked at her, confused. Straight blond hair, blue

eyes, long legs, toothpaste-commercial smile. Alice *had* to be a popular girl.

"Actually, I guess I *am* a freak of nature," she said, almost to herself. She seemed proud of it. She smiled and took a bite of her sandwich.

"What are you talking about?" I asked.

She put down her sandwich. "I'm a duck."

"Huh?" I looked for some sign she was about to burst into that familiar Jensen laughter. But she didn't.

"I'm a beaver. A Labrador retriever."

"What are you talking about?" I asked. For one very small moment, I was afraid Alice was about to reveal herself to be a total lunatic. It would be an uncomfortable paddle home.

"I have webbed toes!" she exclaimed.

I stared at her in disbelief. "For real?"

She nodded. "I suppose you want to see."

"Well, yeah," I admitted. It occurred to me that I'd never seen her barefoot.

Alice pushed off her left shoe. She wiggled her toes at me. They were different, definitely. The extra skin between them made her toes look a little short. But she didn't look like a duck.

"That's not so bad," I told her. "I wouldn't say freaky or anything."

"Ha," Alice retorted.

"It's kind of, I don't know, mermaidy," I volunteered.

"Adam. We're talking toes. Not fins."

"But you look great. No one's going to notice a little extra skin between your toes."

She looked at me for a moment. I felt my face turn red. Out of kindness, I think, she looked away. She stared out across the water. "Yeah, well, try telling that to the flip-flop girls," she said.

"Flip-flop girls?" I couldn't help laughing. It seemed like a perfect way to describe the girls like Emma, Margaret, and Annie back home. "We have some of those at my school, too."

"I hear they're everywhere," she said. "They're plotting to take over the world." Now she was smiling. She pulled her sneaker back on. "Back you go inside your cage, you little monsters," she said to her foot.

That got us both cracking up. "OK, that was weirder than your toes are," I told her.

"That's all right," she said. "I kind of like weird."

She ate three cookies and stood up. "Ready to paddle some more?"

I nodded. We packed up the remains of our lunch in the grocery bag and stowed it in the canoe. Alice had me climb in first. Then she lifted the bow and eased it off the mud, gliding the canoe into a few inches of water before stepping inside.

"Where'd you learn how to handle a canoe?" I asked her.

She pushed off the riverbed with her paddle. "Camp Watson," she replied. "Camp of freaks."

"Everyone has webbed toes?" I asked.

"I knew you were going to say that. No, it's for girls like me who like S-C-I-E-N-C-E. We spend all day solving mysteries, cracking codes, splicing genes."

"Splicing genes?"

"Just making sure you were listening," she said.

"You still haven't explained your boating skills."

"This is Minnesota, Adam. If they didn't teach you ten thousand lake sports at summer camp, they could be accused of child neglect. Even at Geek Camp."

"I believe that, actually," I told her.

We began paddling upstream, slowly now, with the laziness that comes after a good meal in the warm sun.

"So, what *do* you do all day?" Alice asked me. "Since you're not watching TV or playing computer games."

"I don't know. Like I told your mom: swim, canoe, play cards . . ." It wasn't a very exciting list. I was tempted to lie and tell her I was building a small sailboat or rewiring the cabin's electricity. Instead, I confessed, "I guess I spend a lot of time sitting around. Lying in the hammock. Sketching comic strips — that kind of thing."

"Ooh, comic strips! That sounds interesting," Alice said. "Are you working on a book or something?"

"No, nothing that impressive," I said. "But I invented this superhero for myself the other day, since I'm the only one at the cabin with a fully functioning brain." I told her about how I'd come up with the idea for Memory Guy and the ways he would save people from their bouts of forgetfulness.

"Would he swoop in and help kids if they blanked out in the middle of a test?" Alice asked. "Now that could be useful."

"Or cheating," I said.

"Ha! Good point!" she said. "But I like this Memory Guy thing. It's geeky, but it's got potential."

I couldn't tell if she was being serious, but I accepted it as a compliment. We drifted into a comfortable silence again.

The river was quiet and empty along this stretch. We passed a green heron clinging to a partially submerged branch, eyes fixed and back hunched like a new kid at school hoping to escape notice. When I pointed this out to Alice, she said if he didn't want to be noticed, he probably shouldn't be wearing yellow leggings.

"Or a green poncho," I added. "Actually, he's dressed a lot like the kids in our high school's marching band."

"For real?" Alice asked.

"They wear green coats and yellow pants. School colors," I explained.

"Spiffy," Alice said. "Are you in band?"

"I'm learning trumpet," I told her. "But I think I'll stick with jazz band. They let you wear black and white."

We could have kept paddling for longer; after a few more miles, the Potato River emptied out into Potato Lake. But when we hit a stretch of river so shallow we had to get out and walk, we decided it was time to turn back. Alice pulled the bow of the canoe around while I guided the stern. The cool river water bubbled in through the hole in my sneakers.

"My parents are probably approaching level-five worry by now," Alice said.

"On a scale of . . . ?"

"Six."

"Then maybe you should call them," I said.

Alice shook her head. "I can't."

"Doesn't your cell phone work out here?" I asked.

"I don't have a cell phone," Alice said.

"Yes, you do — in your shorts pocket," I said.

"Good one, Memory Guy," Alice said. "But, really, I just brought this." She reached into her pocket with her free hand and pulled out a little pack of Kleenex. "It's much more useful than a cell phone. And much quieter, too."

I grinned. Alice wasn't quite what I'd expected.

Once we were back paddling with the current, it didn't take us long to reach our lunch spot. I spotted a couple of our footprints in the mud. As if reading my mind, Alice pointed toward them and said, "Aren't those duck prints?"

"Ha-ha," I said. But I liked the fact that we'd left our mark on the site, however impermanently. "We should call it Duck Island from now on," I told Alice.

"Only if you promise not to tell why."

"Deal," I said.

We passed through the marsh into the open water, which had filled up with fishing boats, sailboats, and even a couple of pontoon boats. It felt like a crowd after the emptiness of the river, but Alice didn't seem to mind. She gave a friendly wave to the occupants of every boat we passed.

"Do you guys ever water-ski up here?" she asked me.

"No way," I said. "Grandma hates speedboats. She says they're so noisy she can't hear the loons."

"Well, that's true," Alice said. "I never thought about that before."

When we reached Alice's dock, both of her parents were there, scrubbing the steps even though there didn't seem to be anything on them.

Mr. Jensen stood up. "Hello, sailors!" he called cheerfully. "We thought maybe you two had paddled to Lake Superior!"

Mrs. Jensen gave us a smile, but there was a worried look in her eyes. "You must not have had cell service out on the lake," she told Alice. "I called half a dozen times."

I felt like I should make excuses and explain where we'd been, but Alice just laughed. She hopped out of the canoe, then knelt and held it for me while I made my way to the bow seat.

"See you, Memory Guy," she whispered.

"Later, Duck," I whispered back.

I gave her parents a polite wave and headed home.

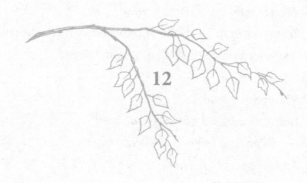

12

"THERE YOU ARE," my mother said when I finally arrived back at the cabin. She was shelling peas at the kitchen table. "I would have gotten worried if I still thought you were out there on your own."

I poured a glass of lemonade and didn't say anything.

"Mrs. Jensen called midday when she couldn't reach Alice on her cell phone. You didn't say you were paddling with her."

"You didn't ask," I said. I put the glass down on the counter and started to walk away. "Did Dad call while I was out?" I asked.

"I thought he called you already," she said.

"He missed this week," I told her.

"Surprise, surprise," Mom said, shelling away.

I hated the sarcasm in her voice. "He probably had to work late," I said. "Not everyone gets to work when and where they feel like it." I headed back to my room before she could say anything more.

To my dismay, I spotted another note in the mirror over my dresser. I opened it and began to read.

My love,
Dottie and I wear our eagle hats and
march around town. But where are you?
And when will I tell her our plans? Will I
or won't I will I won't I . . .

The note drifted off like that, and this time she hadn't even signed her name. What year did Grandma think this was? She'd made those eagle hats as a teenager! And did she really think she'd go back to the Fourth of July parade next year . . . with my grandfather?

I threw the note in my sock drawer, wishing I'd never seen it at all.

After dinner, Grandma and I played checkers while Mom finished up the dishes. Grandma had been so much more animated with Dottie around — as if seeing an old friend had really woken her up. But in her notes, she seemed to be reliving the sad times when my grandfather was away, or the moments when her life wasn't settled. If her brain was wandering back in time, why didn't it wander back to the best and happiest moments, like the ones Dottie loved to talk about?

"Grandma," I said as I slid my checker piece forward, "was Dottie Lewis at your wedding?"

"Dottie?" she asked. "Of course she was. She was one of my bridesmaids!"

"So she knew my grandfather," I pointed out. I hardly knew what to call him.

Grandma looked at me like I was the crazy one. "Well, if she was one of my bridesmaids, you would think so, wouldn't you?"

"I'm just asking, Grandma," I said. "I thought you said something once . . ." I hesitated.

"What?" Grandma asked.

"I don't know. Something about how you couldn't tell Dottie about the two of you and your plans." My voice tightened. I was wandering out onto thin ice.

"I wonder where you heard a thing like that!" Grandma said. "Dottie Lewis introduced me to your grandfather — they were second cousins. Of course, that doesn't mean I told her all the little details of our court-ship. In fact, I'm sure I didn't. But why would you care about a thing like that?"

"I don't know. Never mind," I said. Grandma jumped two of my checker pieces. I looked up at her. "But those must have been happy times. When you were getting married to your best friend's cousin. It's almost like you and she were becoming family!"

"Of course," Grandma said.

"Did you do crazy creative things? Like at the Fourth of July parade?" I asked, still determined to help her remember the good stuff. But Grandma just shrugged.

"I'm not sure we were very crazy or creative by then. But the wedding cake was delicious," she said, which should have come out sounding like a happy memory but somehow did not.

"Did I hear someone say wedding cake?" my mother asked as she strode in. "What are you two talking about?"

"Nothing," I said.

"Nothing at all," said Grandma. "I'm tired. And I'm going to bed." She stood up creakily and headed off to her room.

My mother looked at me for an explanation, but I just folded the checkerboard into a *V* and concentrated on sliding all the checkers back into their box.

13

"ANYONE FEEL LIKE A WALK in the woods this morning?"
Mom asked at breakfast. "There's a nice breeze coming
across the lake. It shouldn't be too buggy." It had been
two days since Dottie's visit, but Mom still sounded
cheerful, and she and Grandma were getting along better. Maybe we needed to invite visitors over more often.

"Sure," I said.

"I think my old bones can manage a little mosey,"
Grandma said.

We started out down an overgrown path that led
past a forgotten outhouse.

"You really used that thing?" I asked Grandma. It was hard to imagine having to make such a long trek in the dark of night just to pee.

She gave me one of her looks.

"We all did," Mom said. "Especially when we had lots of family visiting. I always ended up out this way in a tent with a bunch of cousins."

We crossed a broad grassy clearing that looked out on the lake below. Butterflies spiraled among the tallest flowers. Grasshoppers sprang out of our way as we walked.

"We should have picnics here or something," I said, admiring the view.

"It's where Grandma had her wedding reception," Mom said.

"That again," Grandma said, almost to herself.

There didn't seem to be any obvious path out the other side of the meadow, but Grandma acted like she knew what she was doing. She stepped over a fallen log, and soon we were back under the trees.

"There used to be a slew of trails out here," Mom said. "Ma and I kept them clear all summer. What was that stuff we sprayed on the poison ivy?"

"Something you can't buy anymore," Grandma said.

"Probably totally toxic," Mom said.

"You turned out OK," Grandma retorted.

Through the trees, we heard the drumming of a woodpecker, and it grew louder as we continued on our trail. "Where is it?" I asked.

Grandma pointed her hand up ahead to the right. I saw a flash of red, then something popping around the trunk of a tall red pine. "Is it a downy woodpecker, Grandma?" I asked.

"Hairy," she corrected.

"I don't know how you keep all those birds straight," Mom said, pushing her hair out of her eyes.

"When you really care about something, you don't forget," Grandma said.

"I wish that were true for me," Mom said. "I've forgotten so many things I used to know."

"Like what?" I asked.

My mom thought for a moment. "I can't remember!" We all laughed.

I was afraid Mom was going to start a serious conversation about my grandmother's memory, but instead she said, "Think you can get us back to our road, Ma?"

Grandma nodded and tromped on. I wasn't sure she really did know her way. We were out there for a long time, stepping over logs and through brambly shrubs, weaving in and out among the trees before we finally hit the dirt drive. But I liked her confidence. It was like watching an old dog in the woods: she seemed perfectly happy to be wherever she was in that moment. When we reached the road, Mom breathed a sigh of relief.

"Phew! It's getting warm again!" she said, pushing up her sleeves. "How are you doing, Ma?"

Grandma didn't say anything. She looked completely exhausted now that we were on the open path. It was hotter with fewer trees overhead, and though the footing was easier, she moved much more slowly. When we reached the cabin, Grandma sank into the built-in bench on the deck. Mom brought us all lemonade.

"I hope I didn't wear you out too much, Ma," my mom said.

"I love those woods" was all Grandma said in response. After she drank her lemonade, she leaned her head back and stared out at the trees, not saying a word.

Still warm from the walk, I changed into my swim trunks and went down to the lake. Instead of walking the length of the dock and jumping in, I waded straight in from the shore. I swear I could feel the water making contact with every bit of my skin, pore by pore. Then I dove under and let myself be enveloped and buoyed by the cool lake water. I swam and somersaulted and dove some more, feeling like I might never want to get out of the lake again.

A pair of loons was swimming along the long edge of Grandma's property. I swam over toward them, keeping my head above water and moving as slowly and quietly as possible. They knew I was there. Periodically they'd dive underwater and reappear in some unexpected place, swiveling their heads each time to see where I was. But they didn't seem terribly concerned. Probably they knew a scrawny city kid was no real threat. And, in fact, the third time they popped up, I could have sworn they'd come closer. I could see individual feathers and water droplets glistening on their backs. The loons' bodies seemed more massive and barrel-like up close than they did from a distance. We bobbed along for a while at the water's edge, diving and resurfacing, eyeing one another with curiosity.

Finally the loons had enough of me. They dove down and resurfaced far out in the lake, and I made my way back to the dock. As I pulled myself up the ladder, I spied what looked like a giant black donut making its way in my direction across the shallow water. It was Alice, lying in her inner tube and kicking her way over from her dock to mine.

"Ahoy!" she shouted. She was holding a parcel in one arm, keeping it raised above the water.

When she reached the dock, she handed me the bag

and slid off the tube into the water. Then she popped up again and pulled herself up onto the dock.

"What's this?" I asked, peering inside.

"More cookies. From my mom!"

"What for?" I asked.

Alice shook the water off her skin. "I think she was just so relieved you got me home alive!"

"Wow. She has seriously low expectations," I said.

Alice sat down on the edge of the dock, and I joined her, passing the bag of cookies over in case she wanted one, too.

"Didn't you get any grief for being gone all day?" she asked.

"Not really," I said. "Your mom called, so my mom knew I wasn't out there alone."

"Your mom is so cool," she said.

"Er," I said. "Not so sure about that one."

"I like your grandma, too," Alice said. "Although she's a little intimidating. My mom wasn't at all sure about introducing herself the first time. She'd heard the stories. . . ."

"The stories?" I asked. I hated to think what stories people were telling about Grandma.

"Oh, nothing bad, really," Alice said. "I guess she used to give the neighbors a hard time when they cleared their trees or bought big motorboats. But I think she has a point. She just wants things to stay nice, right?"

"Sure," I said. "But she needs to remember it's not the 1950s anymore."

"Oh, come on," Alice said. "She's not that bad."

"I'm serious," I said. Then I hesitated. I hadn't meant to come so close to the truth.

"What is it?" Alice asked, looking at me with curiosity. She didn't miss a thing.

I glanced behind us to make sure Mom wasn't coming down the dock, and even then I spoke in a low voice. "I'm not so sure my grandma knows what year it is. Not all the time, anyway."

"Really?" Alice didn't sound shocked or scared. Just open and patient — like she was ready to hear more.

It was strangely easy to talk.

"She's been writing these crazy notes," I said. "To my grandfather. Who's been dead since before I was born! She thinks they're, like, college kids again."

"Wow," Alice said. She drew up her knees and wrapped her arms around them. "That's so sad."

"I guess," I said.

"It must be heartbreaking to outlive your husband by that many years," Alice went on. "And to still be missing him so intensely."

"She just seems really, really confused," I said. "In the notes, anyway. She's better in person."

"What does your mom think?" Alice asked.

"I haven't actually told her," I confessed. "I'm pretty sure Grandma only leaves the notes in my room, so Mom doesn't know."

"Really?" Alice said. "Only in your room?" She sounded intrigued. "Maybe she thinks you're your grandfather!" she exclaimed.

"What?" I said.

"I mean, back when he was young," Alice explained.

I stared at her in surprise. "No way," I said, shaking my head.

"Come on, old people mix things up all the time — people, dates. My mom says so, and she should know. It's her job," Alice said. Alice explained that her mom worked with a lot of older patients as part of her nursing work back home. "So do you look like your grandfather? I mean, back when he was a kid?"

"I doubt it," I said. "I don't really know." There was only one picture of my grandfather at the cabin, taken when he was about fifty and had a thick beard. It wasn't a very useful comparison.

"I bet you do," Alice said confidently. "And you've tripped up all her memory wires! Crazy!"

It was a pretty disturbing thought. "I doubt that's

what's happening," I said to Alice. "But if it is, what should I do? Try to tell Grandma that I'm not her dead husband?" I could just imagine how *that* would go.

Alice shook her head. "You said she's better in person, so she probably doesn't even remember writing the notes. So why upset her? I wouldn't even tell your mom, if I were you. She'll find out sooner or later."

"Exactly," I said. It was a huge relief to have Alice in agreement with me on that. "Hey," I said, standing up and eyeing Alice's inner tube. "Want to play aquatic basketball? Or lake golf?"

Alice laughed. "I would — whatever that means! But I promised my mom I'd be home in time for lunch. We made a plan to go *an-teek-ing* in Grass Lake."

"Huh?" I asked.

"Shopping for antiques," Alice said with a grimace. "My mom's obsession. But I'm free tomorrow. How about I come over around this time?"

"Sure," I said. Now that I'd mentioned the lake games, I really wanted to play them.

Alice took a few steps down the ladder, then plopped back onto her inner tube. Getting herself into the right position wasn't easy, and her skin made embarrassing squawking noises as she wriggled awkwardly against the tube. But she just laughed at herself. "This thing needs an outboard motor," she said when she was finally set.

I gave her tube a shove with my foot. "And a muffler, maybe," I added.

"Right," she said.

She smiled and waved, then kicked her way home.

There was leftover pie at lunch and dinner, and I even managed to convince my mom and grandma to play a round of poker with me after dessert. We wagered popcorn kernels instead of money, which was too bad because I won a heap — something I never could have done if my dad or Uncle John had been playing with us.

No notes had appeared in my room all day. For a few sweet hours, it felt like the three of us had finally figured out how to have fun together — that things were going to get better and better now. But that night, not long after I'd fallen asleep, I was jolted awake by angry sounds from the living room.

"No! No! It's not true!"

I heard rapid footsteps cross the hall and got up to follow. In the living room, Mom switched on a light and we saw Grandma at the windows, grasping the sill with her hand like it was a doorknob, turning and pressing, turning and pressing.

"Ma? Ma? What are you doing?" Mom asked, striding over.

"It's not true!" Grandma called, pressing at the glass.

"Ma, you've had a dream," Mom said, reaching out toward her.

My grandmother turned to look at her, and her eyes were startled, far away. "Dottie?"

Mom shook her head. "It's me, Ma. Bobbie. Bobbie and Adam," she said, gesturing in my direction. I gave my grandmother a slight wave.

"We're here at the cabin. You've had a dream."

"No, no, no," Grandma said angrily. "It's not a dream!"

"Ma, please," Mom said. "Let's get back to bed."

"I don't need to go back to bed!" Grandma said. She waved her off, but when Mom put her hand on Grandma's shoulder, she stopped protesting and quieted down.

"Adam, why don't you go get Grandma a glass of water," Mom told me. She guided Grandma back toward her room.

I nodded, glad to have a job. I went to the kitchen and filled a glass with water. By the time I got back to my grandmother's door, my mother was already helping her into bed.

"You can just leave that here," Mom said, gesturing at the bedside stand.

I set the glass on the table. "Good night, Grandma,"

I said, before quickly leaving the room. I went back into my room and slipped under the covers.

When Mom came to check on me, I kept my eyes closed and didn't move. But afterward, alone in the dark, I was awake for a long time, feeling grateful for once that my mom wasn't away.

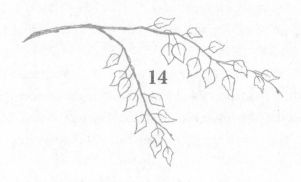

14

IN THE MORNING, Grandma was making pancakes at the stove, just like always. I waited to see if she would say something about what had happened in the night, but if she remembered, she wasn't going to admit it. It was possible that she and my mother had already had a conversation. Neither one was saying a word. Mom busied herself around the cabin, looking distracted and worried. I ate my usual breakfast and headed for the screen door.

"I'm going down to the dock," I called.

Mom nodded, hardly seeming to hear me.

It was going to be another hot July day. The sun glinted off the water, and a pair of mallards winged across the sky. Alice paddled over in an inflatable rowboat, yellow with blue stripes. She was wearing just a bathing suit with a T-shirt over it.

"I'm ready for water basketball or lake golf and a lot of swimming," she said as she climbed up the ladder to the dock.

"Let's start with lake golf," I said. "First we need golf clubs." I headed to shore and scouted around under the pines until I found a couple of stout fallen branches.

"You want to gather the golf balls?" I asked Alice.

"Sure," she said. "Where do you keep them?"

I bent down and picked up a fat little pinecone, dense enough to fly with the proper thwack. I held one up for Alice to see.

She grinned. "Got it," she said, walking off and filling her hands with a mound of small cones. We dumped our supplies at the end of the dock, then I went back to the storage area and found three life jackets.

"These are our holes," I said, holding up one of the life jackets and showing Alice how the head opening formed a perfect circle. "We'll set them out in the water."

"What happens if we miss?" Alice asked. "We can't hit from the water, can we?"

"Nope," I said. "Lake golf is all about the hole in one."

I jumped into the lake and walked the life jackets out into deeper water. "If you miss it on your first shot, it's the other person's turn. First person to get all three shots wins."

"OK," said Alice. "I can handle that."

The life jackets bobbed on top of the water, taunting us as we stood on the dock practicing our swings.

"I haven't been to many driving ranges," Alice said, swinging her pine branch with a graceful swivel.

"You've *been* to a driving range?" I asked. "You'll be fine."

Alice went first. Her first swing missed the pinecone completely. Her second swing sent the pinecone flying straight out across the water, and it came down halfway between two of the life jackets.

"Not bad," I said. I hit my cone hard and watched it land in the water just inches from the closest life jacket.

"You're good," Alice said. She took a few more practice swings and lined up for her shot. This time she hit the pinecone so hard, it flew well over all of the life jackets. "Oops!"

"You're going to take out a loon!" I told her.

She laughed. "I don't know my own power!"

"You might want to switch to your putter," I joked, nodding to her other branches.

"You just take care of your own game," she said.

I placed my pinecone and eyed the middle life jacket, which had opened just slightly and now looked to have the biggest hole. I remembered the way my cousin Rocky kept his eye on the hole until the very last moment when his stick hit the ball. I swung, and the pinecone sailed up in the air and landed directly on top of the life jacket with a humiliating little *plip*.

"That doesn't count, does it?" Alice asked, suppressing a giggle.

I shook my head. "Not unless a dragonfly wants to come by and give me an assist."

"I don't think there are such things as assists in golf," Alice said.

"This is lake golf," I reminded her. "The rules are different."

We played five more rounds before Alice hooked a shot straight into the nearest life jacket. I gave her a high five.

"I knew you'd sink the first one," I told her.

"Beginner's luck," she said with a shrug.

To my relief, I managed to land a pinecone in two different life jackets on my next two swings. Unruffled, Alice hit her second hole in one on her next turn.

"Tie game," I said. I looked down at our pinecone supply. "I think we need more golf balls."

"Let's get those!" Alice said, pointing to the cones

that were now floating on top of the water. She was right — it was a perfect excuse to cool off. We jumped in and rounded up all the pinecones. As it happened, we needed every one we collected and then some, spending the next fourteen turns hitting our shots long, short, wide, and just generally off course. Alice's theory was that the cones had absorbed a lot of water and we hadn't yet adjusted to their new weight.

"Either that or we're thinking too much," she added, preparing for her next turn. She put down her stick, took a deep breath, and stretched her arms up in the air. Then, snapping her four fingers against her thumb like claws, she wiggled her whole torso and shook out her limbs.

"You look like a crayfish," I said. "A weird dancing crayfish. What's with the claws?"

She looked at her hands. "These are castanets!" she said. "I was trying to do flamenco."

We laughed hard — so hard my stomach muscles began to ache. "You really think that's going to help your golf game?" I sputtered.

"Totally," she said. When she'd finally stopped laughing, she picked up her stick, placed her pinecone, took a swing, and sent the cone flying in a beautiful arc. It landed right in the center of her third life jacket hole. She'd just won the game.

"It worked! I can't believe it," I said.

She smiled. "Still want to make fun of my crayfish dance?" She put down her stick. "Now we have to swim again. It's boiling out here!"

We jumped back into the lake and swam until Alice's mother appeared on their dock and shouted that it was time for lunch.

"Hey, want to go canoeing tomorrow morning?" Alice asked before she headed home.

I hesitated. Was it weird for us to hang out every day? Would my mom and Grandma start to tease me about it?

"Please," Alice begged. "My mom's having her new quilting club over for the entire morning. I can't stay home!"

"OK," I said. "I can come over after breakfast."

"Thanks," Alice said. "You're the best."

I had no idea how to respond. It wasn't something anyone had ever said to me before. At least not a girl. "If you say so," I finally mumbled, but Alice was already out of hearing range.

Back in the cabin, Mom and Grandma had just sat down to lunch. If they'd noticed me and Alice on the dock, they didn't say anything about it. In fact, they didn't say anything at all. They just chewed and swallowed, looking tense. Outside with Alice, I'd almost forgotten about Grandma's confusion the night before. But when she went back to her room to nap, Mom cornered me in the kitchen.

"Please sit down for a minute," she said. She lowered her voice. "We need to talk about Grandma."

"What?" I asked.

"What do you mean, 'what'?" she said irritably. "You saw her last night."

I looked at her without responding.

"She was completely delusional!" Mom said.

"She was dreaming, Mom. You said it yourself." I didn't know why I was downplaying what had happened. I'd been freaked out last night, too. But now I felt like defending Grandma—maybe because she wasn't around to speak up for herself.

"I'm worried, Adam," she said. "I've never seen her like that before. Did she behave at all strangely while I was away? Or have you heard her wandering around at night on other occasions?"

"No," I said. It wasn't really a lie. I hadn't actually seen Grandma behaving strangely, and I'd never heard her wandering around at night. I only knew about the notes, and Mom hadn't asked me anything about those yet.

"She did seem better this morning," Mom said. "She doesn't even remember the dream now—or whatever

117

it was." She stood up. "Still, I'm going to call her doctor's office and set up an appointment for when she gets back home."

"That sounds smart," I said, relieved to turn this over to a professional and even more relieved to have the conversation come to an end.

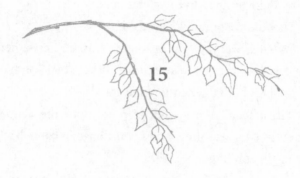

15

I OVERSLEPT the next morning. While I pulled on a shirt and shorts, I noticed a new note sticking in the side of the mirror. Had Grandma snuck into my room during the night to put it there? The thought made me shiver.

This time, I didn't even bother to read the note. I stuffed it into my pocket, grabbed a bagel from the kitchen, and headed outside.

As planned, Alice was waiting for me at the dock, but so was her dad.

"No trips to Superior today, sport," her father said. "We've got a dentist appointment in town at eleven."

Alice frowned. "Sorry," she told me. "I forgot. But can we go out for a little while? The quilters are already here, and they're telling knock-knock jokes!"

Mr. Jensen glanced at his watch, looking amused. "You can take a little spin if you want, but make sure you're home in forty-five minutes max."

That didn't sound like much time.

"What if we met you in town?" I asked her father. "We can dock the canoe at Pullman Park. Then you two can go straight to the dentist from there."

"Great idea!" Alice said, stepping into the canoe. "More time for paddling, and I won't have to come back here at all! Sound good, Dad?"

He hesitated. "Well, OK. I'll meet you at the parking lot. Ten forty-five. You have a clock?"

Alice waved her cell phone at him. This time she wasn't fooling.

We paddled out toward the middle of the lake. On weekdays, we didn't have to worry as much about high-speed motorboats blitzing across our path, so we pulled our paddles into the canoe and let ourselves drift. A bald eagle flew overhead, and we watched as it dropped down, talons first, just a few feet away. It emerged with a flopping fish in its grip and flew off to a tall pine tree over on Grandma's property.

"That eagle knows what he's doing," Alice said.

"Look at your lakefront. It looks like the Canadian wilderness."

I nodded. From here, our shoreline trees formed a dense green margin. You wouldn't have guessed there was a cabin there at all.

"This place is awesome," Alice said. She bent down and nudged a daddy longlegs off her ankle. It climbed back toward me along the inside of the canoe, then folded itself up just under the gunwale.

"How come your parents bought a house up here?" I asked.

"My mom said she thought it would be good for us. Dad gets so stressed out during the year: he's a middle-school counselor."

"Rough," I said.

"And sometimes school is kind of intense for me, too. But, really, I think she just wanted to have another house to decorate."

"She likes that kind of thing, doesn't she?"

Alice nodded. "Antique stores, fabric shops, yard sales . . . She could spend an entire year in places like that."

We stared at the eagle's white head above the pine branches, bobbing up and down as it ate its prey.

"So what's up with your dad?" Alice asked. "Is he ever going to visit?"

"Not this year," I said.

"He doesn't like it here?" she asked.

"He likes it pretty much," I said. "But my parents got divorced last year, so he doesn't get to come. I was supposed to visit him at some point, but it's his busy time at work and I didn't want to leave this place anyway. He gets that."

"Bummer, though," Alice said. "About the divorce."

"Yeah," I said, feeling like I'd said more than enough on the subject. "Should we go?"

We made our way through an inlet filled with lily pads and over to the grassy bank of Pullman Park. We pulled the canoe under a willow tree, then walked up the hill to a picnic table to wait for Alice's dad. It was then that I remembered the note from Grandma.

"Look what I got," I said. "Another note!"

"What's the latest?" Alice asked with obvious interest.

"I actually haven't read it yet," I said.

I unfolded the paper and read it out loud.

G,
*The woodpeckers, the chickadees, the eagles, the
loons. Everyone drumming and calling, and the
woods alive. Leave a message when you can. A
letter makes the day a wonder.*
Your loving V.

"Wow, she's kind of like a poet," Alice said.

"You don't think she's just losing it?" I asked.

"Maybe that, too," Alice admitted. "But I still like the way she writes." She studied the piece of paper. "What was your grandpa's name, anyway?" she asked.

"Randall," I said.

"Randall?" Alice asked with surprise. "Randall doesn't start with a *G*!"

"*G?*" I looked back over the note, amazed that I'd missed such an essential detail. "Whoa, you're right. She wrote *G* not *R*!" I stared at the note, like it was some kind of code that would somehow become legible if I just looked at it long enough. "I must have been thinking *G* for *Grandfather*. But she wouldn't write that, would she?"

Alice shook her head. "That wouldn't make any sense. He wasn't *her* grandfather."

"At least it's not an *A*," I said, relieved. "But who's G?"

We sat in silent speculation.

"Guess what," Alice said with a smile. "Granny has a boyfriend!"

"*Had* a boyfriend," I corrected her. "Remember, she's writing like she's in the past."

"Still," she said. "She had a secret love! You should ask your mom if she knows who it could be."

"Maybe," I said. That didn't sound like the kind of conversation Mom and I would have.

"Are you going to write her back?" Alice asked.

"What? Who?" I asked.

"Your grandma! You should write her back. She asked for messages," Alice pointed out.

"No way!" I declared. "I don't even want to read these anymore. They're starting to give me the creeps."

"Oh, come on," Alice said. "It's so sweet. And mysterious."

"Easy for you to say," I said. "She's not leaving them in your bedroom!" I folded up the note and stuffed it back in my pocket.

"By the way, don't feel bad that you didn't pick up on that clue," Alice teased. "You didn't go to Camp Watson."

"Yeah, yeah, show-off," I said. "Anyway, can we change the subject? I really don't want to talk about my grandmother's love life anymore."

"I think it's cute," said Alice.

"That's because you're a girl," I told her.

"Yeah. So?" she said.

Just then a car pulled into the parking lot. We looked over, thinking it might be Alice's dad. But instead of the Jensens' Subaru wagon, it was a shiny SUV. Four high-school girls in sunglasses spilled out, tennis racquets in hand. Three were blond; they all had long, straight hair in ponytails and wore shirts and shorts in pastel colors.

"Ugh," Alice said.

"What do you mean, 'ugh'?" I asked. "They look just like you will in a couple of years."

Alice shot me a look. "Oh, come on."

"Seriously," I told her. "You give me all this Camp Watson geek talk. But I bet you're a total tennis star!"

"What's wrong with tennis?" Alice said, somewhat defensively.

"Wait — you really are, aren't you?" I said incredulously. "You're an all-star, popularity-contest-winning tennis player!" I'd meant to be teasing her, but it hadn't come out that way.

"I'm not!" she exclaimed. "What are you so worked up about?"

I shrugged. "Every time I see a pack of girls like that — dressed all the same, peering around with their hotshot sunglasses — it creeps me out," I said.

"I'm not a pack of girls," Alice said. "I'm just me."

"I know," I told her, feeling suddenly foolish. "Sorry."

Alice looked like she wanted to say more, but just then her father's car pulled up. "I guess it's time for my appointment," she said. "You OK getting the canoe back by yourself?"

"Sure," I told her. I might not have been any stronger than I was at the start of the summer, but at least I could solo paddle pretty well now. "Have fun with the tooth doctor."

"Actually, I'm kind of nervous," Alice said with a grimace. "His name is Dr. Fear."

"*Wah-ha-ha*," I said in my best ghoul imitation, which made her grin.

They drove off, and I walked back to where we'd left the canoe. I stowed Alice's paddle and life jacket and then started the long trip home. There wasn't any wind, and the water was smooth and calm. But it just wasn't the same canoeing on my own.

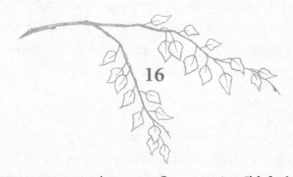

16

THE NOTES CAME in waves. One morning I'd find two
squeezed side by side in the mirror, and another the
morning after that. Then a week would pass with nothing. Grandma had a few more confused evenings, but if
it hadn't been for the notes, I might have thought it was
just typical old-person stuff. I was tempted to ignore the
notes, to toss them in the trash without reading them
and pretend that everything was normal. But Alice
wouldn't hear of it. She kept the entire collection, reading and rereading them for clues about who the mysterious G was. I told her to stop wasting her time, that
whoever he was, he was an old man by now — maybe
just as forgetful as Grandma. Either that or dead. No

matter what Grandma wrote in those notes, I doubted she'd actually want to see him now even if she could.

There was only one note I didn't show Alice right away. I found it in the mirror one night in July after Mom and I returned home late from dinner and a movie in town. Grandma had insisted on staying back at the cabin, saying she'd rather listen to her old records than see a loud Hollywood movie. She was already asleep when we got home.

G,
You know I don't care how strong you are. A little
shy. My strange enchanted one. Love you and
be loved in return, that's the greatest. You're my
nature boy.
Viola

As usual, the note blended words and ideas together in ways that made no sense to me. Alice always insisted that we just didn't understand Grandma's mind well enough — that if we could get inside her memory, the notes would seem much more coherent. But one thing was clear even to me: whoever G was, he wasn't anything like my tree-felling grandfather. Not so strong? A little shy? G didn't sound like Paul Bunyan at all. If anything, he sounded like he could have been a dock-sitter.

I tucked the note away in the back of my sock drawer, trying to sort it all out. If Grandma had been so crazy about a shy nature boy, why did she always tell me and my cousins we had to be tough and strong like my grandfather? And was Alice actually right all along about the reason Grandma left the notes in my mirror: did I remind her of this guy, G?

The thought made me a little embarrassed, so it took me a few days to share the note with Alice. When she finished reading it, she said, "Nature boy. Ha!" and gave me a knowing look. But thankfully she left it at that.

Then one day in late July, there came a note that I knew I had to show Alice right away. Sharing it with her would be like handing a dog a rib-eye steak. I made my way over to her place and waited impatiently for her parents to finish doing some work around the yard. As soon as they disappeared inside the house, I handed Alice the note.

My love,
So many months have passed now — I've given
up all hope of finding your gift for me, your secret
treasure. I don't know if I can ever forgive you for

being such a tease. Now it's just one more part
of you I've lost forever. Can't you come back . . .
somehow? Can't you come home?
V.

Alice's eyes widened as soon as she hit the magic word.

"Treasure?" she exclaimed.

"*Secret* treasure," I said.

"What do you think it is? Gold? Jewels?"

I shook my head. "That's the first thing I thought of, too. But let's be real. We're talking about Grandma and her teenage boyfriend, not a pack of pirates. It was probably a book of love poems or something lame like that."

"It's so tragic," Alice said. "But I wish she'd tell us more. Really, Adam, you should try talking to her sometime. Or writing her notes. We need more information!"

"No way," I said, remembering how awkward it had been even trying to find out more about her engagement. "She's confused enough as it is!"

Alice sighed.

"But should we start looking for the treasure?" I asked. "I mean, it might be interesting to find it, even if it isn't worth anything."

Alice's brow furrowed. "That was — what did you

say? — more than sixty years ago? What are the chances it's still here after all these years?"

"You never know," I said. "There are bottles of iodine in my grandma's medicine cabinet that look like they've been there half a century."

But she had a point. Grandma had been puttering around the cabin for her entire adult life. Between her exploring and my mom's cleaning, somebody would have turned up a hidden treasure long ago.

"It could even be underground," Alice said. "Buried treasure." She shook her head. "This is going to be a tough one, Sherlock."

"Memory Guy," I corrected.

"Oh, right. Except that's not going to help us much at this point, right? You can't remember something you never knew."

"Memory Guy has his limits," I acknowledged. "But if you want to know the names of all fifty states in alphabetical order, say the word!"

Alice smiled tolerantly. "Listen, I'm going to go put this note with my collection. Then let's take a dunk, OK? It's hot out here."

I nodded and watched her jog toward her house. When she came back out, she was wearing her swimsuit and holding a rainbow-colored towel.

"Last one in is a dead walleye!" she said, throwing the

towel onto a lawn chair and dashing off toward the lake.

Before I'd even taken off my sneakers, Alice had run the length of the dock. She looked over her shoulder and shook her head when she saw how far behind I was. Then she did a cannonball into the lake, sending a huge spray of water over the dock. She popped up, waving and laughing.

Grandma's secret treasure was kind of interesting — I couldn't pretend it wasn't. But the real mystery of the summer was how a guy like me was getting to spend an entire summer hanging out with a girl like Alice.

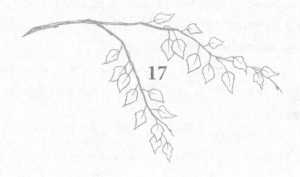

17

MY UNCLE MARTIN came up to visit the first weekend in August. He was a nice guy — big and gentle, with long wiry hair pulled back in a ponytail. He taught history at the University of Minnesota, teaching and writing year-round, so he was ready to make the most of his brief time at the cabin. As soon as he arrived, he took off his shoes and didn't put them on again all weekend unless he was going out for a bike ride. He stayed outside as much as possible — encouraging Mom and Grandma to eat dinner on the deck, and even sleeping in the meadow in his own tent. And he told me he wasn't going to read a single word on a computer while he was there.

"I get so sick of being indoors and looking at a glowing screen," he said. "This place is like a balm for my wounds."

We were sitting on the deck eating cheese and crackers. A chipmunk darted back and forth on a log below us, and a blue jay called out a warning from overhead. Mom was making a pasta dish in the kitchen, and Grandma was nowhere to be seen.

Uncle Martin cut a couple of slices of cheese and handed one over to me. "How's your grandmother, Adam?" he asked.

"You're asking me?" I said.

"I trust you more than Bobbie," he said.

I gulped, feeling a wave of guilt. "She's OK, I guess," I told him.

He didn't say anything.

"She gets a little confused sometimes. Don't all old people?"

Uncle Martin popped a cracker in his mouth and shook his head. "Not everyone," he said. "You should see this fellow in my department. Herman Milstein. He's been retired for twenty years. Twenty years! But the guy still comes to his office every day, fills his coffee mug, and gets to work. His work is careful and smart — and it's still being read by scholars in his field."

"Well, it's hard to compare that to Grandma," I said. "But she still remembers her birds and everything."

Uncle Martin nodded. "I think your mom's overreacting, actually. She feels so guilty that she's not around to help out with things more — in St. Paul, I mean. But Ma and I, we have an understanding. If she doesn't fence me in, I won't lock her in a cage."

"A cage?" I asked.

"An old folks' home. Assisted living, or whatever they call it these days. A place like that would kill your grandmother."

Just then, Mom came out with a pile of plates and four forks. "Adam, honey, can you go in and get the glasses?"

I wondered if she'd overheard us. I headed inside and was halfway to the kitchen when I saw Grandma coming out of my room, patting her pockets.

"Grandma?" I said. "Everything OK?"

She looked distracted but she told me, "Everything's fine."

"Grandma, you didn't . . . ? You didn't leave me a note, did you?"

She looked at me quizzically. "What do you mean, 'note'?"

"Those notes, Grandma," I said, already wishing I

hadn't said anything about them. "You leave them in my room sometimes."

"I don't know what you're talking about," she said, setting her mouth in that firm straight line.

I walked past her into my room and looked up at the mirror. No note. I sighed.

"Sorry, Grandma," I said. "Never mind."

"You're as bad your mother," she said haughtily. "I don't know why everyone's so suspicious around here."

"Sorry," I mumbled again.

I went back to the kitchen and got the glasses Mom had asked for. Grandma held the door for me, and I carried them out to the table.

"Now, how about getting that pasta?" Mom said.

"You sure work that boy hard," Uncle Martin said, giving me a sympathetic look.

"You call that working hard?" Mom said indignantly.

I was a little worried that she and Uncle Martin were going to start arguing, but when I returned with the pasta, they were both smiling.

"Uncle Martin has a surprise for you, Adam," Mom said.

I found myself bracing for the announcement. Surprises made me uncomfortable.

"What's that?" I asked.

"I bought myself a new bike for my fiftieth birthday,"

Uncle Martin said. He gestured across the driveway to where his bike was leaning against his car. "This is my old one," he said. "It's covered a lot of miles, but it's been a loyal and safe steed. And your mom tells me you've outgrown your bike back home. Would you like to have mine?"

"Me? Sure," I said, even as I wondered if I was really big enough to ride the thing. "Thanks a lot, Uncle Martin."

"Maybe you can take it out to visit Alice," Mom said with a teasing smile.

I didn't answer her. I tried to think about water glasses and pine needles or anything else that would keep my ears from turning red. But then Uncle Martin asked Mom and Grandma if they'd heard the one about the doctor, the lawyer, and the ice fisherman, and all eyes shifted to him. Like I said, Uncle Martin was a nice guy.

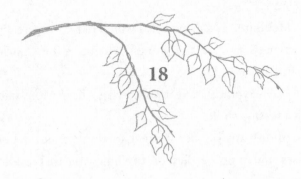

18

UNCLE MARTIN LEFT the next day after lunch. Mom settled in at the kitchen table with a pile of manuscripts, and Grandma looked like she was going to do more of her wayward puttering, so I decided it was time to try out my new bike. I was glad it was a mountain bike; a road bike with narrow tires would never have held up on the rutted drive out to the main road. Once there, it only took a few minutes to get to Alice's street and her short paved driveway.

"Cool bike," she said, coming out of her house to greet me. "Is it your birthday or something?"

I shook my head. "My uncle Martin gave it to me last night. It's his birthday, actually, so he's giving himself a new one."

"Lucky you," Alice said.

"Want to ride out on the rail trail?" I asked. I'd always been jealous that my great-grandfather had been able to take a train from the Twin Cities to the cabin in his day. Those trains didn't run anymore, but somebody had had the bright idea to convert some of the rail lines into paved bike trails. You could ride for miles out there as long as you didn't get tired of looking at cornfields.

"We didn't bring my bike up," Alice said. "But I'm pretty sure one got left behind by the old owners. Let me go see."

She ducked into her garage and came out with a bike that looked at least two sizes too small for her. It was hot pink with sparkly streamers coming from the handlebars and had a little white basket in front covered with plastic flowers.

"Don't say anything," she said.

"You think you can ride that?" I asked. "It looks like it's made for a kindergartner!"

"It'll work," she said with cheerful confidence. "Once I put some air in the tires, anyway."

"What about a helmet?" I asked.

"Yes, Mr. Boy Scout," she said. "Give me a minute."

She disappeared back into the garage and emerged with a Dora the Explorer helmet perched on her head.

"You've got to be kidding me," I said, cracking up.

Alice tried to pull the helmet down, but it wouldn't budge. "I guess I am kidding," she said. She thought for a moment. "Wait! I know what I can use!"

She returned to the garage. This time she came out wearing a huge black hockey helmet, complete with a face guard.

I burst into laughter again.

"I guess the people before us played ice hockey, huh?" Alice said behind her face guard.

"I guess," I said. "I never met them."

"Hermit," Alice said. "You're as bad as your grandmother."

I ignored the comment. Alice found a pump, and we filled the tires of her bike. Then she fastened on her hockey helmet.

"So are we ready?" she asked.

I gave her a thumbs-up. "I think you'll be *very* safe."

With that, we pushed off—me on Uncle Martin's cool blue mountain bike; Alice wearing red high-tops and a gargantuan hockey helmet as she rode a little girl's pink bike.

We pedaled out to the rail trail and followed it up and down the rural hills. We hadn't thought to bring snacks or money, so on the way home, we were crazy with hunger. Talking about food only made it worse, so I finally changed the topic.

"Name the four worst things about your school," I said to Alice.

"In Minneapolis?" she asked.

"You have another school?" I asked.

"No." She laughed, almost to herself. "It just seems so far away right now."

"Well?"

"I hate cafeteria food," she said with a shudder. "The beef macaroni, the tofu supreme. Even thinking about it now makes me totally lose my appetite."

I grunted in agreement.

"I also hate school dances — they're so awkward, with all your teachers watching you like you're a lab rat in some kind of menacing experiment."

"All of middle school is a menacing experiment," I told her.

"I hate the edges of the hallways," Alice went on. "That's where the wax hardens and the janitors never clean it right, so there's all this dust and lint and gunk stuck in there . . ." She fell silent.

"What's the fourth?" I asked.

Alice hesitated. "I'm really bad with the pressure," she said finally.

"The pressure?" I asked, confused. Given how much Alice talked about science, my first thought was that she was talking about air pressure. The kind barometers measure.

"I get stressed out. Big-time, sometimes," she said, almost like a confession.

"You?" I asked.

"Why are you so surprised?" she asked. But of course I was surprised. Here at Three Bird Lake, she seemed cool as a cucumber — fearless and unflappable.

"It's different for boys," she said, not waiting for a response. "The girls at my school, there's a bunch of them trying to be the smartest, have the cutest clothes, have the most friends, get the starring roles in the school play. It feels like what everyone notices isn't how many things you're doing right but whatever thing you're not doing perfectly. To me, anyway."

"So you freak out sometimes?"

"Yeah," Alice said.

"Not here, though," I said.

She shook her head. "It's totally different here," she admitted.

"Back in Minneapolis you wouldn't wear an over-size hockey helmet while riding a little kid's bike, would you?"

"Are you kidding?" she asked, grinning again.

"It actually looks kind of cool, you know," I said.

"Try telling that to the flip-flop girls," she said for the second time that summer. And of course I knew just what she meant.

That night at dinner, my grandmother peered at me with sly interest, the way she had on our first morning at the cabin.

"You sure are spending a lot of time with that Jensen girl, Adam," she said. "I told you you'd like her."

Mom glanced at me, seeming both curious and a little concerned. I tried to shrug them off.

"She *is* the only person within two decades of my age around here," I pointed out.

"She's also very sweet," Mom said.

"You never had a boyfriend up here at the lake, did you, Bobbie?" my grandmother asked.

"Just one," Mom said. "Alex Pinkwaller. His dad owned the soda fountain, remember? I think I only went out with him for the free ice-cream sundaes."

"Alice isn't my girlfriend," I told Grandma.

"She didn't say she was," Mom said. "Right, Ma?"

Grandma shrugged. "You can't fool me."

It was something she had said a lot over the years,

with a smug tone that drove me crazy. "You can't fool me because I'm older, wiser, and more clever than all the rest of you combined"— that was her basic message.

"Well, what about you, Grandma? How many boyfriends did you have up at the cabin?" I asked her. I said it a little viciously, I'll admit. But why couldn't I ask? Why was I so busy protecting her from her own secrets if she was letting me in on them anyway, knowingly or not?

A shadow passed over Grandma's face.

"Oh, Adam," Mom said. "There was only your grandfather. You know that. Dottie introduced the two of you when you were, what? Seventeen? He always said it was love at first sight."

"That's right," Grandma said. She sounded genuine enough, but I knew better. Maybe it was love at first sight for my grandfather. But not for Grandma. There was something faraway in her eyes right then; I was sure of it. I wished Alice were at the table with me now to confirm it.

"I miss Dad," my mom said.

Grandma nodded but didn't say anything.

It was weird how fast their moods could change. The air felt heavy with memory or sadness, or both. I offered to wash the dishes just to give myself a break from it. But Mom said she was in a cleaning mood, which was like a fish saying it was in a swimming mood. I was happy to oblige, and escaped to the dock.

The light was already getting dim beneath the trees, but out on the lake, it was silvery and sweet. Gentle waves chuffed against the dock, but when a fishing boat crossed nearby, they rose through the wooden slats, splashing the bottom of my sneakers.

Alice appeared on her dock. I waved and thought about shouting a greeting. But with the fishing boat gone, things had settled into a twilight quiet I didn't want to break with my voice. Alice seemed to understand. She disappeared briefly and returned a moment later with her inflatable boat, which she paddled effortlessly across the water. When she got close, I tied it to a post on our dock and gave her a hand up the ladder.

"Grown-ups doing dishes," she said quietly. "Excellent time for escape."

"Here, too," I said.

We stood beside each other on the edge of the dock, staring out across the lake and not saying a word. It was the best kind of silence.

A pair of loons drifted nearby, and we watched them for a long while without moving. I wondered if I was seeing the same pair every time or whether there were different families coming through. After a while, I spoke to Alice in a whisper. "I always think if I stand here long enough and quietly enough, I'll get to see them do something really amazing."

Alice eyed the loons with curiosity. "Like burp?"

I rolled my eyes. "Well," I said, "sure. Anything could happen. What do we know about loons, really?"

Alice nodded, then turned and took a slow 360-degree view of everything around us. Suddenly she squeezed my shoulder hard and gestured back toward shore. "Look!" she whispered.

I scanned the shoreline in the direction she was pointing. And then I saw them. Threading their way through the shoreline vegetation on the long side of Grandma's property were two small animals. Their fur was a glossy chocolate brown, and they had long, slender bodies that seemed almost to undulate as they walked. They were mink, I thought. I'd never seen one in the wild before; I hadn't even known there were any around the lake. Fortunately for us, they were in no particular hurry, but just zigged and zagged along the shore, occasionally darting close to the water, then away. When they reached the dock, they passed easily beneath it, then reappeared, closer to us than ever. We could see their tiny ears and the whiskers on their muzzles. It was tempting to walk back down the dock for an even better view, but I knew that would just startle them away. Eventually they trotted across the wet sand toward the scruffy vegetation in the direction of Alice's property. We followed them with our eyes as long as we could, frozen in place and hardly daring to breathe. When they disappeared entirely, Alice released her grip on my shoulder.

"Oh, my gosh!" she exclaimed. "Did that just happen?"

I knew what she was feeling. My whole body felt jolted, awake. I couldn't have even explained why.

"Were they weasels? Otters?" Alice asked.

"I'm pretty sure they were mink," I told her.

"As in mink coats?"

"That's one way of putting it."

"Have you ever seen them before?"

"Only stuffed ones," I admitted. "At the natural history museum."

"Wow. Coats. Stuffed. It's like they're usually only seen when they're dead," Alice said. "Poor mink."

"Not these ones, though," I said. "Can you believe it? They live out here with us, and we didn't even know it."

"It kind of came true — what you were talking about," Alice said. "We stayed quiet long enough, and we saw something really, really incredible."

"Better than a loon burp, that's for sure."

Alice smiled, then scanned the length of Grandma's woods. "I wonder what else we're missing," she mused.

"We should go on a wildlife hunt sometime," I said.

"Definitely," she agreed.

Alice glanced up at the sky. It was growing dark now, and we both knew she had to go. She climbed down into her boat.

"Good night, Adam," she said. She paddled a few strokes, then peered into the shoreline trees. "Good night, mink," she called softly, then paddled away.

I lingered on the dock with the night and the loons and the memories of the mink and Alice, in no hurry to give up any of it and go back inside.

19

I RETURNED TO THE LAKE early the next morning, dimly
hopeful that the mink would be back. I wandered along
the shoreline, retracing their path, and noticed a trail of
tiny prints in the wet sand where they had walked. But
of course the mink were gone to wherever it was that
mink go.

My stomach growled, and I headed back into the
cabin to see about breakfast. Inside, Mom was stuffing
dish towels into a large cloth bag.

"I'm going to the Laundromat this morning," she
told me. "Do you need anything from town?"

I shook my head.

"Maybe you can give Grandma a hand," Mom said. "She's organizing her shelves a little."

"Maybe," I said.

Mom frowned, clearly disappointed by my answer, but I ignored her.

After Mom left, I could hear Grandma opening and closing drawers in her room on the other side of the kitchen wall. I sat down to eat cold pancakes and flipped through a two-week-old copy of *Sports Illustrated*, wishing I'd asked Mom to buy me a new one. Still, reading old news was better than the alternative, which was staring at the spice rack. Almost an hour passed before I looked up and saw Grandma wander into the living room. She had a small stack of papers in her clutches.

"It's like this every year," she said with a scowl. "The doctors leave the paperwork to the last minute, and we end up being the ones to put it in its place."

"What doctors, Grandma?" I asked.

"At the hospital. They get all the credit for their medical smarts, but they wouldn't be anywhere without us nurses picking up all the pieces."

My stomach twisted. Grandma hadn't been a nurse since before I was born. "Do you still have paperwork from those old days?" I asked.

She shuffled the papers in her hands, looking perplexed. I came over and peered down at them. What I saw didn't look like hospital paperwork — just some old letters and bills. My stomach twisted again. She'd never been this confused before.

"Don't worry about that stuff, Grandma," I said. "Those are just old papers of yours."

Grandma frowned and glanced at them again.

"Maybe you've done enough cleaning for one day," I said.

Grandma looked at me quizzically. "I think so," she said. "I don't know. Help me put these away, anyway."

I hesitated. What I really wanted was to slip back outside and pretend this conversation had never happened. But I was used to following her orders, so I reluctantly agreed. As she led me to her room, her shoulders looked narrow, almost fragile, beneath her shirt — like the bones of a small bird.

"That's where the office folders go," she said, pointing to a filing cabinet in the corner of the room. She handed me the papers, then sat down on her bed and began fussing with a buttonhole on her shirt.

I pulled open the top drawer of the filing cabinet.

"You make sure those get where they belong," she said.

I looked down at the stack of papers. On top was a letter from my mom, written when she was in college. Underneath it was a heating bill, and, beneath that, a bill from a doctor dated 1978. That must have been what had set off her confusion about the old nursing days. The rest just looked like more of the same.

I began to slip the papers into folders, more eager to be done than accurate. "Medical" looked like a good-enough place for the doctor's bill, and "Utilities" seemed right for the heating bill. I propped open a folder called "Personal" and was about to slide my mom's letter inside when I saw a large envelope labeled "Map." Curious, I peered inside and saw a folded piece of yellowing paper.

I glanced at my grandmother. She was dozing off now, her chin resting on her chest. I slipped the paper out and unfolded it. It was a hand-drawn map. Across the top were the words "Viola's Treasure Map." I didn't recognize the handwriting.

My heart took an extra beat. Was this a map from Grandma's mysterious boyfriend? Could it really have survived all these years? Keeping the map in my hand, I slid the file drawer closed and left the room. It wasn't until I was outside and down the drive that I let myself take a closer look.

"Viola's Treasure Map," I read again. And below that: "with loony love."

The map was written in black ink in very careful handwriting. About two-thirds of the way down was a neat rectangle with a zigzag line beneath it. At the top was a small target symbol labeled "Secret Treasure!" Connecting these two points were a series of dotted lines labeled with animal street names: Deer Drive, Beaver Boulevard, Raccoon Road, Hare Highway, and more. After each name was a number of steps — for example, "Deer Drive: 200 steps." At the bottom of the map was a compass — the sort you'd find on any ordinary map.

I had to tell Alice. Biking was slow-going on the long, rutted drive, and I didn't feel like dragging out the canoe. Instead, I headed straight into the woods. The shrubs grew thick between our cabin and Alice's house, so I had to wrestle with a bunch of branches and take a lot of detours. But finally I broke out of the trees and found myself standing at the top of Alice's driveway. I trotted down the length of it and rang the doorbell.

"Adam! What a pleasant surprise!" Mrs. Jensen exclaimed, opening the door. "We were just sitting down to cinnamon rolls. Would you like some?"

Even though I'd already eaten breakfast, I wasn't about to turn down cinnamon rolls. "Uh, sure," I said. Then, as if it were an afterthought: "Is Alice home?"

"Of course she is! Come in, come in."

It was the first time I'd stepped into Alice's place. It was a small house, with wood paneling on the walls and a soft green carpet on the floor. The kitchen had a homey feel, with lace curtains on the windows, canisters with painted fruit on them, and lots of framed sayings made out of cross-stitch on cloth. I knew what they were because my mother had tried to make her own cross-stitch one summer, to fit in better with the town ladies. Her saying was "Don't Put Off Till Tomorrow What You Can Do Today," but she never got further than "Don't Put Off."

Alice was sitting beside her father at the kitchen table, chomping on a cinnamon bun.

"Well, look who's here!" Mr. Jensen bellowed.

"Hi, Mr. Jensen," I said. "Hi, Alice."

Alice gave me a slight smile, and for the first time in my life I thought I could actually pick up on a secret signal — the kind girls sent all the time but we boys never understood. It was like she was apologizing for her dad and refusing to greet me enthusiastically in his presence. But I could tell she was happy to see me. I really could.

"You've got to have one of these cinnamon rolls," she said, pointing at the tray of pastries on the table. "Mom has a rare talent."

Mrs. Jensen had already put a roll on a plate for me, and I took the empty seat across from Alice.

"I hear you and Alice had a wildlife experience yesterday!" Mr. Jensen said. "Mink, huh? You sure about that? There are a lot of raccoons around here. They get into our garbage more often than I care to admit."

"They weren't raccoons," I said confidently.

"What about a couple of stray cats?" he continued.

"They weren't cats, Dad!" Alice exclaimed.

Her father seemed to consider this. "You sure they weren't skunks?"

"Dad!" Alice said.

Now he was just teasing, and I didn't mind so much. My dad sometimes teased me in the same way.

The cinnamon roll was delicious, but I couldn't wait to get Alice alone so I could tell her what I'd found. Unfortunately, Mrs. Jensen sat down with a cup of tea and seemed to be settling in for a good long conversation.

"So, Adam, how much longer will you all be staying up here?" she asked.

"Um, I think we're supposed to go home the week before Labor Day. But my grandma wants to stay longer. She says the fall is even better than the summer."

"I'd love to come up in the fall sometime," Alice said. "No bugs. Glowy leaves. Can we come up some weekend, Mom?"

"I don't see why not," Mrs. Jensen said.

"We'll just need to make sure to fire up that furnace!"

Mr. Jensen said gustily, rubbing his hands together. "It'll be cold here on the water!"

Before Mrs. Jensen had a chance to ask another question, I stood up awkwardly. "Thanks for the cinnamon roll, Mrs. Jensen. But I need to go, um, do something."

Alice looked at me quizzically. I'd hoped she'd pick up on my secret signals the way I'd picked up on hers, but she just seemed confused.

"Going mink hunting, maybe?" Mr. Jensen asked.

"Maybe," I said distractedly. I looked at Alice and gave a slight nod toward the door. She glanced at the door, looking more confused than ever. Telepathic communication was never going to be my thing.

"Or maybe treasure hunting," I said in a moment of inspiration.

Alice's eyes widened. "Hey, hold on — I'll come with you." She stood up and brushed cinnamon roll crumbs off her hands.

"Call if you're not going to be back by lunch!" Mrs. Jensen said as we hurried to the front door.

"What is it?" Alice asked the moment we were out of earshot. "Did you find another note?"

"Even better," I said, drawing out the mystery.

When we reached the end of the driveway, I pulled the folded paper from my pocket. "Would you have any interest in looking at a . . . treasure map?" I asked.

"No way," Alice whispered. "For your grandmother's treasure? Is it from G?"

I nodded and held it out for her to see.

"Where did this come from?" Alice asked.

"My grandma had it in a file drawer," I explained. "She asked me to put away some papers, and that's when I saw it."

"So you stole it?" Alice sounded more pleased than disapproving.

"Well, I'd prefer to call it borrowing," I said, happy that I'd managed to impress her.

We sat on the grass and studied the map. Alice marveled over every detail — from the ink (she informed me it was from a fountain pen) to the penmanship (she told me no one writes like that anymore) to the dotted lines with their animal street names. She even admired the carefully drawn target symbol — three concentric rings — with the "Secret Treasure!" label.

"This is so awesome, I think I'm going to scream," Alice said at last.

"Please don't," I said. "Your father will come out with a shotgun."

Alice bit her lips as if to contain her voice. Then she looked at me with shining eyes. "What are we waiting for?" she asked. "We have treasure to find!"

"But we don't know where to start," I pointed out.

157

"Sure we do," she told me. "At the rectangle!"

"Yeah, yeah," I said. "But what's the rectangle?"

Alice laughed. A lifetime of analytic genius and Camp Watson summers had come to her aid. "It's your cabin, dummy!" she said. "Didn't you notice the waves on the porch railing?"

The zigzag line. The waves. Of course!

I sighed in reluctant admiration. "OK, Duck," I said. "Lead the way."

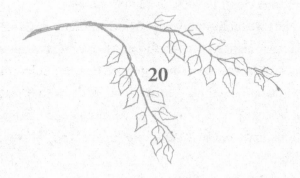

20

WE SHOULD HAVE KNOWN it wouldn't be that easy. Surely Grandma would have recognized that the rectangle was the cabin. And like any good outdoorswoman, she was handy with a compass. I don't know why we thought we'd be able to solve in an afternoon a mystery she'd been working on for decades. But we did.

We started at the corner of the cabin indicated on the map — the northeast corner, facing the lake. I hoped Grandma wouldn't get a sudden urge to step out on the deck; we'd have a hard time explaining what we were doing skulking around under the cabin on such a nice day.

Alice held up the map. "First up: fifty steps on Mouse Main Street!" We stood shoulder to shoulder and walked fifty paces straight away from the corner of the cabin, parallel to the lake. I ended up a step ahead of Alice, which we decided was probably OK, since my paces were closer to what an adult's would be.

Next we took twenty paces down Chipmunk Chute, heading straight to the lakeshore. After a ninety-degree shift, we were ready for thirty steps on Beaver Boulevard.

"Maybe we should mark our path with bread crumbs or raisins or something," Alice suggested, "so we can look back and make any adjustments if we think we were off."

I liked the idea of trail markers but wasn't interested in going back into our cabin. So instead I proposed we use sticks to mark our intersections. Alice agreed and began gathering medium-size sticks to poke into the ground every time we turned onto a new trail.

"Next is Mink Meander," I said. "It looks like a forty-five-degree angle, doesn't it?" I wondered why G bothered to draw a compass when he didn't even refer to it in the directions.

We started counting off forty paces but found ourselves at the water's edge by the time we'd counted to thirty-two.

"Do you think we go in?" Alice asked.

"I guess," I said. "Maybe the water level has changed after all these years."

I pushed my sneakers off and waded eight steps into the water. "What's next?" I asked Alice, who was on shore, holding the map.

"Head straight back to land," she said. "Two hundred steps on Deer Drive!"

I started counting, and when I reached shore, Alice handed me my sneakers and joined in. Two hundred paces was a lot, and we ended up walking straight past the cabin and entering the woods.

"Using steps as your unit isn't exactly scientific," Alice commented.

"His mistake, not ours," I said.

We continued with the rest of the map trails. We ended up angling back through the high meadow where Grandma had had her wedding reception, then far back into the forest where Grandma, Mom, and I had walked a few weeks before. When we counted our last step, we looked down at our feet and saw, well, nothing. Just more trees and bare ground and a fallen log.

"Do you think we're in the right place?" Alice asked.

I shrugged. "Let's look around."

At first, we searched along the ground for anything that looked like it might be important. Scattered among the leaves were sticks, acorns, mushrooms, rocks, and a fresh pile of deer droppings. But we didn't see anything that looked like a special treasure from decades ago.

Alice was, not surprisingly, a tenacious searcher. When we'd covered all the open ground, she began turning over rocks. Then she squatted down on one side of a fallen log and peered inside. "Hand me a stick," she said. When I did, she began jabbing it in as far as she could reach.

"I really hope you're not blinding some poor baby chipmunk," I said.

She frowned. "It feels more like rotten wood." She went over to the other side and tried again. "This would be better with a flashlight."

I looked at the map again and at the concentric rings marking the treasure's spot. "Do you think maybe he drew a target on the ground where he buried the treasure?"

Alice wrinkled her forehead. "If he did, I doubt it would still be here." She stood up. "Maybe we're not in the right place," she said. "What if we tried the whole thing again, but this time with my paces instead of yours?"

"Why?" I asked.

"Maybe my paces are closer to your grandmother's."

"If anything, I think we should try longer paces. I'm sure he was taller than me or Grandma."

"OK," Alice agreed. "We'll do it again and take extra-long steps. But if we end up in the center of town, don't blame me!"

We made our way back to the corner of the cabin where we'd started. We could see where we'd left the sticks at our intersections before, and it's true that we ended up following a different path when we used longer paces. But with all the zigzagging, we ended up closer to our first ending point than I would have predicted.

"Interesting," Alice said. "Maybe we should just cover a big circle that includes this spot and our last spot. And we'll go over it with a fine-tooth comb."

"That's still a lot of ground to cover."

"We have a lot of time left at the lake," she said. "If there's treasure here, we'll find it."

I didn't want to talk about how much time we had left at the lake. It happened like this every year — just as you rounded the bend into August, and the deerflies died off, and the water temperature was at its most perfect, and the crickets began their nighttime percussion, you had to start thinking about heading home. And this year, maybe even more than any of the others, I wanted summer to last forever.

"What if he just made her a batch of cookies or something?" I said. "A treasure like that would be long gone by now."

Alice shrugged. "Maybe. But let's look some more anyway."

We searched the ground for a couple of hours, with a quick break for lunch. After a while, I found I wasn't looking for anything anymore, just poking idly at the forest floor, swatting at bugs, thinking about the lake.

"Are you still looking?" Alice asked.

"Sure," I said.

"Liar."

I stood up and wiped my brow. "Fine. You got me," I said. "How about a swim?"

Alice shook her head. "Are you even thinking about your grandmother?"

"What do you mean?" I asked, startled by the question. In truth, the treasure hunt felt like a game for me and Alice, not my grandmother's concern. Not anymore, at least.

"Wouldn't she be touched if we found her secret treasure?" Alice asked.

I made a face. "I don't know what she would think, actually." It occurred to me then that I really had no idea who my grandmother was at this point: a judgmental lady who made me feel bad about my paddling skills, a lovesick teenager who wrote poetic notes to her boyfriend, a confused old woman who struggled to remember what year it was. More and more she seemed almost like a puppet whose voice changed depending on who was holding the strings.

"Let's just take a little break," I told Alice. She was kneeling in the dirt, her hands raking through the grassy undergrowth.

"OK," she said, squinting up at me. "But only if you promise me one more search day. At least."

"Deal," I said.

An hour later, we were swimming in the lake in the late-afternoon sun. I saw a canoe working its way across the water in our direction, with two people inside. It was Alice who recognized them first as my mom and grandmother.

"Hello, there," Mom said as they approached. "We wondered where you two had gone off to."

Grandma smiled smugly at me from beneath her bucket cap. As they drew up to the dock, she shipped her paddle and grabbed hold of the dock with a gnarled hand. But Alice was already there to help them come to a stop, standing waist-deep in the water and holding the canoe steady while they climbed out.

"Thank you, dear," Grandma said.

"Yes, Alice," Mom said. "Very thoughtful."

I dropped under the water before Mom could give me a pointed look.

When I popped up, Alice was helping Mom carry the canoe onto the shore. They were chatting as they turned the canoe over, and still talking as they made their way back to take the paddles from Grandma. Then the three of them walked the paddles and life jackets up to the storage area under the cabin and disappeared from sight.

I turned and swam freestyle down the length of Grandma's property, pulling hard against the water with my arms and kicking steadily. When I neared the boundary to the church camp, I didn't even feel tired. I turned around and swam back at full speed. Alice was waiting for me on the dock.

"I should probably be heading home," she said.

"OK," I said. And then I couldn't help myself. "Did you have a nice chat with the ladies?" I asked.

"Adam," she said, as if it were a complete sentence.

"What?" I asked.

She cocked her head to the side and looked at me just the way Grandma did sometimes — knowing and amused.

"Am I not supposed to talk to them?" she asked.

"Of course you can talk to them," I said. "I'm sure it thrills them. For a lot of reasons." I pulled myself out of the water and padded over to my towel.

Alice followed me. "You sound paranoid," she said.

"You don't know them like I do," I said. "They pry

and try to find out as much as they can about you. And then all they do is laugh at you."

Alice looked at me without saying anything. This time, I couldn't read her thoughts. Was she feeling guilty for divulging something private between us, or was she thinking about what I'd said?

But it looked like I wasn't going to find out. She started climbing down the ladder and said simply, "We talked about Camp Watson." And then she swam home.

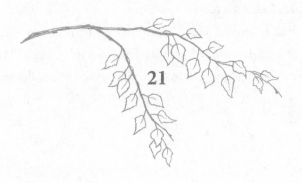

21

THE NEXT DAY, Alice showed up as planned for another round of treasure seeking. We didn't say anything about how we'd left things the day before, and I was glad to put it behind us.

The day had a muggy, heavy feeling to it, which seemed to inspire the bugs to new heights of activity. It was a lousy time to be in the woods. After walking through our paces two more times — once with Alice's steps and then once more with mine — and searching the ground like a pair of bloodhounds, we felt the futility of our hunt settle in.

"It's miserable out here," I said, slapping at a bold mosquito trying to pierce me through my eyebrow.

"This map is really annoying, actually," Alice said, inspecting it again. "It doesn't have any landmarks besides the cabin. And it's crazy not to use real compass coordinates."

"No wonder my grandmother sounded frustrated in that note," I said. "Remember, she called him a tease."

"He *is* a tease!" Alice said. Just then light raindrops began falling. We heard them hit the birch leaves over our heads before we could feel them, but we figured it was only a matter of time before we'd be getting wet.

Alice carefully tucked the map inside her shirt. She'd been smarter about the bugs than I had, throwing on a long-sleeved red-checked shirt over her T-shirt. "There's so much we don't know," she said with a sigh.

"No point in getting wet, anyway," I said. "Do you need a ride home in the canoe?"

She shook her head as we began walking back to the cabin. "I've been bushwhacking more and more through the woods. Pretty soon I'll have a regular path beaten down through all the poison ivy."

"You can call it Poison Ivy Parkway," I said.

"That's beautiful," Alice said sarcastically.

We stood under a lone oak tree by Mom's and Grandma's cars. Alice gazed at the cabin with a thoughtful expression. "People were so charming back then, weren't they? Can you imagine a guy today making a hand-drawn treasure map for his sweetheart?"

"He wouldn't even call her his sweetheart," I said.

"Good point," she said. "And then naming the paths after animals. It's so old-fashioned and cute. I miss the old days."

I laughed. "You weren't even there."

"That's why I miss them," she said. She looked up at the treetops and spun around slowly, almost as if she were trying to wind back time with each turn of her body. But then she stopped and shook her head and gave me her usual smile. "So we're done treasure hunting?" she asked.

"I think so," I said. I was actually relieved to be ending our search. What had started out as a fun diversion had turned into a lot of frustration.

"Can I keep the map a little longer, anyway?" Alice asked. "I thought I might go over some of your grandma's letters and see if there are any clues in them."

"Sure," I said. "And do you want to do something later? I could teach you cribbage."

"Oh, um," she said, looking uncomfortable, "I can't. My dad and I are . . . doing something."

"Yeah?" I asked, hoping she'd explain.

But all she said was, "Yeah. So another time." She

walked around our woodpile and began to pick her way through the enveloping trees down Poison Ivy Parkway.

The rain continued as just a light sprinkle, so I didn't hurry back inside. Instead, I leaned against the tree and looked at the cabin, trying to imagine going back in time twenty, forty, sixty years. How different would things have looked back then? Aside from the cars, there wasn't much here to indicate the year. Just my mom's New Balance running shoes on the deck, my fleece jacket hanging up to dry. But the cabin was the same. The trees were the same — taller, Grandma said, but still the same. The clothesline, the light fixtures, the rubber bucket where we washed the sand off our bare feet before stepping indoors — I was pretty sure these had been here, virtually unchanged, since the day the cabin was built. That was part of Grandma's master plan. But wasn't there still something else around us — some hum of activity, pushing and pulsing in the air, that we could feel standing here even if we couldn't see it? Maybe it was our communications signals, buzzing around us. Or maybe it wasn't the present at all, but the past and all its stories living on in this place — not buried and forgotten, but racing around unseen like a pack of ghosts so that we crashed into them at every turn without even quite knowing it.

* * *

During lunch, I tried to ignore the tense conversation that had started up between Mom and Grandma. Not surprisingly, Mom was fixated on the calendar, trying to figure out how to get everything done before we left and trying to resolve what to do with Grandma. Just as predictably, Grandma found her tiresome.

"Martin can come get me like he always does," she told Mom. "I don't know why you keep bringing this up."

"Because, Ma, you can't stay here alone until he comes. Look at you — have you driven the Taurus even once this summer? How will you get food?"

Grandma shrugged.

"Maybe she could get weekly deliveries," I suggested.

Mom shot me an angry look, so I went back to my silent eating. But I couldn't help feeling a little protective of Grandma. I remembered what Uncle Martin had said, about how she didn't fence him in and he wasn't going to do the same to her. Why was it just my mom who wanted to make everyone follow certain rules?

I peered through the screen window and noticed that we still hadn't had a downpour. No wonder the atmosphere felt so charged.

"I'm trying to reason with you, Ma," Mom said. "But at a certain point, I'm just going to make you do what I say. You know that, don't you?"

My grandmother looked up at my mother with a

sudden flash of anger. "You're treating me like an infant! This is my house, Bobbie. If I want, I can make you leave!"

"Don't be ridiculous," Mom said. She picked up her dishes and half tossed them in the sink. Good thing they were made out of metal. "This is what I get for trying to take good care of you. Beautiful."

Ladies fighting. I hated it and felt a sudden longing for the old days, when my dad and uncles and cousins were around to fill the house with silliness and energy. Dad would know what to say to calm them both down, or at least he would have before he and Mom started their own arguing.

I left the kitchen, grabbed some money from my room, and told the two of them I was going into town. Mom and Grandma weren't even talking anymore, just brooding from opposite sides of the cabin. Never was I more grateful to Uncle Martin for the gift of his bike.

22

THOMPSON'S DIME STORE had emptied piggy banks all over Hubbard County for decades. Kids loved the place: the squirt guns, beach balls, yo-yos, plastic tomahawks, cheesy paint-by-number sets. Supposedly Mr. Thompson had opened the store at a time when many things did sell for just a dime. Now the name was sort of a joke; even the windup tarantulas cost a dollar. But I didn't care. It was still my favorite store in town.

The bells chimed when I went inside, and the familiar smell of scented candles filled my nose. I turned to the toy and game section and started looking around.

The jigsaw puzzles were usually tempting, but not these—too many soft-focus scenes of kittens and unicorns. I checked out the bins of plastic animals, packages of marbles, dart sets, playing cards. The amount of junk was impressive.

The only thing that really captured my interest was a rubber crayfish, its antennae and pinchers hilariously wobbly. It reminded me of how Alice had looked dancing on the dock the day we'd played lake golf, and I couldn't help chuckling.

Then something else caught my eye. It was a black plastic chest about the size of a small shoe box and filled with fake gold coins and colorful gems. Pretend treasure, of course, for kids who were into pirates. But it got me thinking about what Alice had said, about how nobody ever made treasure maps anymore. Maybe I could bury a treasure chest and make a map showing her where to find it. And unlike G, I'd make sure my map was easy to follow.

I looked again at the plastic chest. It would be kind of fun making a map and figuring out how to give her clues. But I'd need to fill it with something other than fake gems and gold—with something Alice would actually like. Then I remembered that the candy store usually sold coin-shaped chocolates covered with gold foil. I could fit a bunch of them in the chest. Maybe I'd even throw in the rubber crayfish. Alice would think it was hilarious.

I bought the treasure chest and the crayfish from the salesclerk — an older teenager who looked at me like I was two instead of twelve.

"It's not for me," I mumbled as he slid my purchases into a paper bag.

"Whatever," he said.

I made my way down to the candy store and bought gold coins for Alice and a bag of malted milk balls for myself.

It was still early in the afternoon, and I didn't have any interest in getting home before dinner. So I headed over to the grocery store and spent the last of my money on a couple of new magazines. There was a bench at Pullman Park right next to the water and under the shade of the weeping willow. It was the perfect place to waste some time. I rode over to the park, propped my bike against the tree, and sat down to read and munch on the malt balls.

After an hour my mouth felt sticky and parched. I walked up the embankment toward the water fountain, halfway between the kids' playground and the tennis courts. Someone had left pink gum stuck to the edge of the metal basin, but I ignored it and took a few big gulps of water. When I was done, I wiped my mouth with the back of my hand and was just about to return to my bench when I caught sight of a familiar figure on the tennis courts.

It was Alice.

She had her hair pulled back in a smooth ponytail and was dressed entirely in white — white dress, white tennis shoes, and white wristbands. She looked like she'd just stepped out of a sports catalog.

On the other side of the net was a guy — about fifteen — dressed in a slightly more rumpled version of the same outfit. He had that old-school preppy look, where the clothes looked super expensive, but he was too cool to keep them neat.

So this was her afternoon plan. And it wasn't with her dad at all!

I watched as Alice gathered up some balls — rolling them deftly up against the side of her foot with her tennis racquet, then sliding them onto the racquet to lift them to her hand. She tucked the extra balls under her dress — what did she have, pockets in her underwear? — and then positioned herself on the baseline. Her movements were seamless as she drew back the racquet, tossed the ball into the air, and then whacked it powerfully over the net. Mr. Preppy had no trouble returning it, but Alice ran to the net and smashed the ball into the front corner, where not even a pro could have reached it. Her opponent said something that sounded sarcastic, but Alice was already picking up another ball and jogging back to the baseline.

It was then that she spotted me. For a moment, she hesitated, but then she waved her left hand eagerly in my direction, as if my catching her playing tennis with a country-club guy was the most normal thing in the world. I was glad we were too far apart to exchange words, too far even, I hoped, to see each other's expressions. I waved halfheartedly, then headed back for my bike.

A sparrow sat perched on my bag from the dime store. It fluttered away when I approached but left behind a piece of white bird poop that summed up perfectly how I now felt about the treasure chest and my stupid idea for making Alice her own map. What a fake she was, pretending to be some kind of down-to-earth nature geek with freaky toes and a love of science. In truth, she was what I'd always suspected her to be: a star athlete who hung out with preppy guys and who, once she was back home, would probably joke about the dorky guy she had to hang out with all summer.

I picked up both bags and dumped them into a garbage can. Then, rethinking it, I reached into the one from the dime store and retrieved the rubber crayfish. I grabbed a stick off the ground and used it to bang every bench and bin in my path as I pushed my bike up the hill. Who was that preppy guy, anyway? I wondered. Alice's boyfriend from the tennis team, visiting for the weekend? A friend of the family from the wealthy, suburban side of Three Bird Lake?

As soon as I reached the parking lot, I tossed the stick and hopped on my bike. Maybe I heard my name being called as I rode away; maybe not. It didn't matter anyway.

23

I PEDALED OUT to the main road to the cabin, then cut onto the rail trail and biked as hard as I could, up and down the tree-lined hills. When the path opened up through fields, the sun was almost unbearably hot and the air was so thick, it was hard to breathe. But sweating felt good, and I ignored my growing thirst to make it a marathon ride.

I reached the town of Dalton, where I found a drinking fountain and stretched my legs. When I turned back for home, the sun was a fuzzy yellow ball sinking down through the gray gloom. The fast ride out seemed to have drained some of my fury. I pedaled more slowly now, left with a feeling of disgust. As if I'd been tricked or let down. It reminded me of when I found out my favorite Cubs player — the guy who seemed so righteous for as long as I'd followed him — had actually been using steroids just like so many other players. How were you supposed to believe anyone in this world, if you couldn't believe the ones who seemed the greatest?

I almost felt like crying, which only made me madder. *Come on,* I told myself. *Alice is just a girl. And it isn't like we're best friends or anything. Who cares if she's been lying about who she really is?*

But I knew that it was more than that. Alice was also hope, in a way. Hope that someday I really could understand girls and be friends with them. Or even something more. And now that hope had been crushed.

My legs were aching by the time I turned onto the dirt drive to Grandma's cabin. Going over the bumps and roots sent shock waves up my arms to my elbows, so I kept my eyes trained right in front of my tire to choose as smooth a route as possible.

That's why I didn't see Grandma's station wagon until I was almost upon it.

The car was stopped in the middle of the drive, angled awkwardly to one side, with the front end smashed into the trunk of a stout tree. I stopped, shocked by the sight of the car here in the road, and shocked by the damage. I peered through the window on the passenger side, but there was no one inside.

I rode quickly to the cabin. Mom's car was there, but there was no one around. Not even a note. For once I regretted the ancient technology of the cabin, which didn't even have an answering machine. I also regretted not having my own cell phone, because Mom surely would have tried to call me. She carried hers sometimes, but I knew her well enough to know that she probably hadn't kept it charged out here at the cabin. Still, I used the phone in the cabin to try the number, just in case. When it went straight to voice mail, I hung up and tried my dad at work. He didn't answer, either, but I left a message asking if he'd heard anything.

The cabin had never felt so empty — or so isolated. I wandered from room to room, looking to see if there were any clues to explain what had happened. But all I found was one of Grandma's notes stuck into my mirror. I'd probably missed it that morning. The first part was written in blue pen:

> G,
> *All I want is to be with you forever.*
> *Viola*

Scribbled at the bottom in pencil, she'd added:

P.S. Who is the old lady?

I threw the note in my drawer, no closer to knowing what had happened that afternoon. Had Mom made Grandma prove she could drive? Had Grandma fled in a huff? And how badly was everyone hurt? I thought about going back to the car and looking to see if there was any blood on the steering wheel, but I couldn't bring myself to actually do it. Besides, I wasn't even sure the windshield had been cracked. Maybe they hadn't hit that hard.

I wandered onto the deck and peered through the trees. It was unnaturally dark for this time of day, and a wind was picking up. The tree branches shuddered. I wrapped my arms around my body and tried to get a better view of the sky. As I suspected, tall dark clouds were gathering to the north. Just my luck. Here I was, all on my own at the cabin for the first time in my life, and it looked like we were about to get a serious storm. For a moment, I thought about running down Poison Ivy Parkway to the comfort of Alice's house and family. But not after what I'd seen that afternoon. No, that path was a dead end. I was on my own.

I found a flashlight in case the power went out, made a sandwich for my supper, and sat by the phone. Mom had her problems, but she wouldn't forget about me.

Sure enough, the phone rang just as angry raindrops started pelting the roof. But it wasn't Mom. It was my dad.

"Dad, what happened? Did Mom call you?"

My dad's voice was steady but tense. "Your grandmother had an accident, Adam. They're at the hospital now."

"She was driving? By herself?" I asked.

"I guess there'd been some sort of fight."

I grimaced, thinking of Mom and her needling ways. "Is Grandma OK?"

"She hit her head on the steering wheel and now she's disoriented, but they don't think it's anything too serious. Mom's been waiting around while they get her through X-rays and some other tests."

"Maybe she has a concussion," I said, thinking about football players who banged their heads too hard in games.

"Probably," Dad said. "Anyway, Mom has no idea how long she'll be there. If it starts getting late, she wants you to call your neighbors — the Jensens, is it? — and ask them if you can spend the night over there."

"I don't need a babysitter," I said.

"I know, Adam. But she'd feel better knowing you were with other people."

"I tried calling her cell phone," I told my dad.

"The battery's out," he said. "She says she left the charger at home. But I'm sure she'll try you again soon."

"So why's her car still here?"

"Grandma's car was blocking the drive," Dad explained. "So she hopped in with the ambulance."

There was a long silence after that. Dad and I weren't very good at talking on the phone. A whole summer was going by, and I'd hardly shared any of my news. I hadn't told him about Memory Guy or Grandma's notes or the secret treasure or even Alice. So after a few more strained minutes, we said good-bye and hung up.

I went to the windows and watched the rain slapping the deck. I couldn't get to the Jensens' in this downpour anyway. There was no point in calling — I didn't have anything to say, and the last thing I wanted to do was talk to Alice. Instead, I turned on the radio and listened to a ball game while I washed up the dishes. Even without Grandma here, I could feel her eyes on me. I took the time to dry the plates and put them away.

The phone rang again. This time it was Mom.

"Oh, Adam, I'm so glad you're home now. Did Dad get in touch with you?"

"Yeah," I said. "How's Grandma?"

Mom sighed. "So-so. She's still a bit fuzzy."

"From the concussion?" I asked.

"I'm not sure if that's what it is. We'll be getting test results back in a little while, and then I'll let you know."

"Why was she driving, anyway?" I already half knew the answer, but I wanted to hear it straight from Mom. I was angry at her for treating Grandma the way she had, for leading her to do this.

She sighed again. "She was mad that I'd challenged her independence. She wanted to prove to me that she could drive that old car. I know I shouldn't have spoken to her the way I did. I was just so frustrated."

I didn't say anything.

"After you left, I went back to my room to sort clothes and cool off a little. The next thing I knew, I heard the Taurus starting up. By the time I got outside, she was driving down the drive. And then there was that terrible crash . . ."

Mom's voice cracked, and I could tell she was crying. I held the phone without speaking while she recovered.

"Anyway, have you called the Jensens yet?"

"Not yet," I said. "I can't go over there now anyway."

"Why not?"

"Because it's pouring . . . can't you see?"

"You can't hear or see anything in this place," she

said, meaning the emergency room, I guessed. "It's like a tomb."

I'm sure she regretted the choice of words. Before she got all emotional again, I broke in. "Don't worry about me, OK? I'll be fine on my own till the storm passes over. Just take care of Grandma."

"Thanks, Adam. You really are a great kid, you know that?"

It was a nice thing to say, but for some reason it didn't feel like the right time for compliments.

"Bye, Mom," I said in reply.

The drama of the day was complete when a full-fledged midwestern thunderstorm arrived. Lightning illuminated the dark clouds in surprise bursts, and thunder boomed and echoed so loudly, it sounded as if someone were rolling giant barrels across the sky. I reminded myself that the cabin had stood here unharmed for decades. But for once, being surrounded by tall trees wasn't comforting. I backed myself up against the fireplace, figuring it had to be the sturdiest thing in the cabin. The power went out, just as I'd expected, and I lost the pleasant chatter of the ball game.

The strange part, though, was that I didn't feel afraid. Not about the storm. And not about being alone. It had been terrible seeing Grandma's car smashed against a tree, but even that wasn't what I was dwelling on. Instead, my thoughts kept turning back to the encounter with Alice. The fancy tennis outfit. The guy across the net.

I hugged my knees to my chest and gazed around at the shadows of chairs and tables and lamps. I felt like the Alice I knew was gone, like she'd disappeared. Maybe this was what Grandma felt like so many years ago when her mysterious G went away. Where did he go? Why did he leave her? I wondered if she felt as empty as I did now.

When the storm ended, I could have called the Jensens. But I didn't need to. And frankly I didn't want to. Besides, it was late by then. I turned off the light switches in case the power returned in the night, and went to bed.

24

MOM MAY HAVE LIKED a fresh-scrubbed cabin — the way a space felt open and shiny after she did her work with the vacuums and mops. But for me, nothing beat the feeling of the world after a storm. The clouds had dumped buckets of water over everything, the wind had scoured and polished, and then the sun emerged to make it dry and welcoming again. That's how it felt when I woke up and went outside. The wind was still blowing, curling up little whitecaps on the surface of the lake, but the sun was bright enough to set it all sparkling. I stood on the dock, shivering in air that had turned suddenly cool. We were up north, after all, and by the end of summer, we always felt the first hints of autumn in the chilly air that pushed across the border from Canada.

I decided to make pancakes. Back in the cabin, I rifled through the cupboards looking for Grandma's recipe until I realized that of course she didn't have one. At least not written down. Luckily, she did have an old cookbook called the *Joy of Cooking*, and I followed the directions for their basic pancakes. After I'd mixed in the flour, baking powder, salt, sugar, milk, egg, and oil, it occurred to me to add my own touch. I squeezed in a ripe banana and stirred in a handful of blueberries. Grandma had never put anything like that in her pancakes.

The burner clicked and clicked before finally lighting, sending a burst of orange and blue flames up under Grandma's griddle. I waved the gas smell out of the air, then dropped a spoonful of batter on top of the hot metal. One circle. Then another. My very first pancakes. I was tempted to throw them high into the air when it came time for flipping, but I chickened out. Good thing, because even with the spatula they each landed sideways, sending frothy little batter dribbles onto the pan, which cooked faster than the pancakes they were connected to. I started to scrape the thin parts off with my fingernail, but I burned my finger. Then, while I was running my finger under cold water, the pancakes started to burn. This wasn't going as smoothly as I'd hoped.

I flicked the burnt pancakes onto the counter with a quick turn of the spatula, lowered the heat, and started over. This time the results looked pretty good. When I'd assembled a stack of six pancakes, I turned the burner off and settled down to eat.

Mom called before I was done. "You're there!" she exclaimed. "I talked to the Jensens this morning, and they said you'd never called. What happened?"

"Nothing happened, Mom," I said. "I just didn't feel like going over."

"Is everything OK?"

"Everything's fine."

"Did you find some cereal or something?"

"Nah, I made pancakes." I tried to sound cool about it so she wouldn't overreact.

"Pancakes? Really? Like Grandma? Oh, Adam . . ."

"How is she?" I interrupted.

"Better. They ended up admitting her to the hospital last night. We're meeting with her doctor in about an hour, so I'll find out then how long she's going to stay."

"She has to stay?"

"Just for a little while. I spoke to Mr. Jensen, and he's going to arrange for a tow truck to get her car out of the drive. And Mrs. Jensen offered to pick me up here — maybe around lunchtime. Will you be OK until then? Wait — of course you will."

Her comment took me by surprise. She'd finally been paying attention, the right kind of attention. I felt like saying thank you, but instead I said, "Is there anything you need me to do around here?"

"That's nice of you to ask, sweetie. But I think we'll just figure out our next steps when I get home. Sound good?"

"Sounds fine."

After breakfast I went out into the woods. The ground was damp in places, but the temperature was perfect for hiking. With jeans and a sweatshirt on, I wasn't going to get attacked by bugs. The wind was too much for the mosquitoes anyway.

I rambled out the road past Grandma's car, then cut into the woods to see where I'd end up. Twigs snapped under my feet, and the wind made a ruckus in the treetops. But otherwise it felt as if the voices and noises of the world had dropped away and it was just me and the woods left together. I walked east all the way to the edge of the church camp, then cut across to the bluff above the lake. Walking there gave me the best view — green trees to my left, blue water below. I thought about the mink and wondered if they were down someplace closer to the water, trotting around looking for another meal.

I thought about Grandma's treasure map, wondering where those mysterious lines were meant to be.

When I returned to the cabin, I found Alice sitting on the deck bench, her feet propped up on the wooden table in front of it. She was wearing a red plaid shirt over her jeans and had a black knitted beanie pulled down over the top of her hair.

She looked at me with a steady gaze. "Hi there," she said.

"Hi," I said. "What are you doing here?"

"My dad's out there with the tow-truck guys," she said, gesturing down our drive. "I thought I'd come see how you were doing."

She waited for me to respond, but I didn't know what to say. Was she concerned about me because of my grandma? Or because of what I'd seen in the park?

"I don't really feel like talking," I said.

"Oh." She slid her shoes off the table as if to leave, then bit her lip. "I'm sorry about your grandmother," she said. "My mom says it sounds like the kind of thing she ought to recover from pretty well."

"Yeah, well, we'll see," I said.

"Listen, about yesterday . . ."

"Never mind about that," I said.

"It wasn't my idea, the tennis game," she said anyway. "The kid I was playing against, Drew, goes to my dad's school. He's a delinquent. But my dad bumped into Drew's family in town the other day and said I'd play tennis with him. I think he thought it would be good for Drew." She rolled her eyes. "As if."

So this guy Drew wasn't her boyfriend. I hated how relieved that made me. "I don't care who you play tennis with, Alice," I said to her then.

"Then why are you acting mad?" she asked.

My first reaction was to deny that I was mad, but then I'd be no better than she was. So I said what I really felt. "You lied."

"Lied? About what?" she asked.

"About what you were doing with your afternoon. About being a tennis star."

"So I know how to play tennis. It's no big deal," she said.

"Then why didn't you tell me when I asked?"

"Because you made it *seem* like a big deal. You lumped it together with all those other things, like being popular and being shallow." She sighed and crossed her arms. "Dude, it's just a sport."

She'd never called me "dude" before, and in that moment it rang as falsely as everything else she'd said or done. I'd had enough. I went into the cabin and let the screen door slam behind me. Alice was decent enough not to follow.

25

MRS. JENSEN BROUGHT my mom home in the middle of the afternoon. Sensitive as always, she left quickly, but not before wrapping me up in an ample hug and telling us to call if there was anything else she could do.

Mom looked older. It was clear she'd hardly slept. Her hair was tousled and unwashed, and she was wearing the same clothes she'd been wearing the day before. We walked up the steps to the cabin without saying anything. I expected her to tell me she was going to take a shower, maybe make some coffee, before we sat down to talk. But she didn't. She put down her purse and took a long look around the cabin. Then without even looking at me, she said, "Let's go canoeing."

The wind had quieted since morning, so it wasn't hard to paddle across the open water. Mom took the bow and let me steer wherever I felt like going. I angled the canoe across the water toward the marsh and the river.

The air was still cool, the sky cloudless and so intensely blue that the world had become a giant turquoise marble with us at its center. After we'd found our way through the marsh and onto the river, I finally broke the silence.

"Is Grandma OK?"

Mom turned around, nodded, and gave me a gentle smile. "She's OK. It wasn't a concussion and it's not Alzheimer's. She had a stroke yesterday."

"A stroke?" I asked.

Mom stopped paddling so she could talk, and I controlled the canoe just enough to keep us from drifting.

"A small one," she explained. "We don't even know if that's why she hit the tree, or if the stroke came afterward. But we did learn that it wasn't her first."

Mom said that the tests showed that Grandma had had a series of small strokes in the past — so small they might cause momentary confusion or even a bit of slurred speech, but not necessarily any lasting symptoms.

Still, there was always a risk of a big stroke following one of the small ones, which was why they wanted to keep her in the hospital for one more night.

I thought about the notes Grandma had left in my room and wondered if they were the results of some of those strokes. I felt a fresh wave of guilt about not letting Mom know about them. But hearing about the notes now — and about the mysterious G — wasn't going to do Mom any good.

"Can they give her something so it doesn't happen again?" I asked.

"I think so," she said. "But we'll have to monitor her closely with her home doctor."

"But this is pretty good news, isn't it?" I asked. "At least we know she can get better."

My mother shook her head, then ran her hand over her rumpled hair. "She's still not who she was. I mean, we definitely can't leave her here alone anymore."

I stopped paddling. "You're going to put her into a nursing home?"

Mom pursed her lips. "I don't know. I have a lot to work out."

She looked around at the trees leaning in over the river. A kingfisher swooped down from a branch and glided over the water in front of us before returning to its perch.

"Maybe I've been unfair to Grandma," she continued, speaking slower than she usually did. "She's just so stubborn about things. And she acts so tough. It brings out the stubborn, tough parts of me."

"Stubborn's OK," I said to make her feel better.

"In the right circumstances, I guess," she said with a little laugh. "Anyway, after spending twenty-four hours in a windowless hospital with Mom — sealed in so tight in that white space we didn't even know about the thunderstorm . . . and then coming home to the cabin and all this . . . air . . ." She hesitated.

"It's really OK, Mom," I said.

She wiped away tears. "This place is so alive, and so much of what keeps her alive. Martin's been telling me as much for years, and I just didn't want to see it." She shook her head. "Gosh, Adam, it's going to sound crazy to say this. But I think I resented her relationship with this place. I felt sometimes like she loved it more than she loved us!"

I thought about Grandma's notes and about the parts of her life here that she'd never shared with the rest of us, at least not intentionally. Maybe my mom had good reason to feel a little left out of things. "I know what you mean."

"Or maybe I'm just being silly," Mom said, wiping

away the remains of her tears and sounding more like herself. "But this place is like part of her family. And I really don't want to be the one who rips her away from that. It'd be kind of like pulling the plug, you know what I mean?"

I nodded.

"So," she said, "I have some thinking to do. But in the meantime, we should all enjoy these last days here together. When Grandma comes home tomorrow, I want to be sure she gets out as much as she feels up for. Especially after that hospital."

Mom turned around and we began paddling again, but not in a getting-there sort of way—more like a being-there sort of way. I almost felt as if we were soaking up every sound and sight and smell for Grandma, since she couldn't be here herself.

My mom pointed out a pair of baby turtles warming themselves on a rock. Their shells were shiny and dark green, seeming as new to the world as the day itself.

"I love this place, too, you know," my mom said.

"I know," I said, although I felt it now more than I ever had before.

We talked a little bit then about the details of each of our nights, and I told her about my bold new recipe for pancakes. Mom suggested I try making them for

Grandma the first morning she came back, but then we both agreed that the shock of it might just bring on another stroke. Weird as it sounds, that got us both laughing.

It was nice talking to my mom like that, but that wasn't all I was thinking about. As we traveled, I kept remembering parts of my first canoe trip with Alice — as if the memories were stuck like pushpins to the surrounding terrain. There was the place in the marsh where we'd had to push off the bottom with our paddles, the bend where we'd seen the green heron. When we passed Duck Island, I got lost in a whole mess of memories — about our lunch and Grandma Hattie's cookies and of course Alice's crazy webbed toes.

It was funny to be riding behind my mom thinking about so many things that she didn't know anything about. For the first time in my life, I had my own stories here. Mom, Dad, Grandma, my aunt and uncles and cousins — none of them had been a part of that trip with Alice, and none of them could see what I saw as we crossed these landmarks. It made me feel good for reasons I couldn't even have explained. It also made me miss Alice.

Maybe I was stubborn, too — just like my mom and grandma. The more I thought about it, the stupider I felt about the way I'd reacted to seeing Alice play tennis.

Maybe I'd blown the whole thing out of proportion. Maybe Alice was right. Was it really a big deal that she played tennis like a jock? Wasn't Alice still Alice even when she was dressed in country-club whites?

As we approached the dock, I felt like dropping Mom off and going straight to Alice's house to tell her I was sorry. But Mom asked if I'd mind getting started with dinner while she took a hot shower, and I could hardly tell her no. So I decided I'd just have to wait and visit Alice in the morning, when Mom was busy with other things.

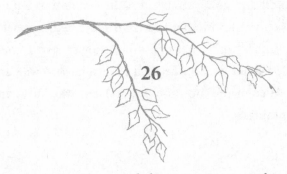

26

AFTER DINNER, Mom said she was going to make a few phone calls, and I was still in a thinking sort of mood, so I put on my fleece jacket and headed to the dock. The sun had already set, and there still wasn't a cloud in the sky; it was a perfect time to watch the stars. I brought down a couple of canoe cushions and lay with my head resting on them.

I took in a deep breath, savoring the crisp freshness of the air and wondering if there was a way to store it up for when we were back in suburban Chicago again. Bottled air. It could become the biggest trend since bottled water. But I didn't really want to sell off any of this; I just wanted to hold on to it for longer.

I sat up and looked to see if maybe Alice had also come down to her dock. But no one was there, and it was growing too dark for a visit across the water anyway.

As I turned back around, I noticed a small dark shape moving toward me on the surface of the water. At first I thought it was a log, but it was too round and traveling with too much control. I realized then that it was an animal, swimming steadily along the shore, creating a V-shaped ripple in the water behind it. It wasn't a mink — too large for that. And too large for a muskrat. As it swam under the dock, I saw the top of its head above the water: eyes and muzzle and nose. Its dark body, just visible beneath the surface, was impressively large — large enough that I felt a quick rush of adrenaline at its being so close to me, even though of course it had no interest in me. It might not even have known I was there.

As it swam past and away, I could just make out a fat, flat tail. That's when I knew for sure what it was. A beaver!

I watched until the beaver head became a tiny dot and then faded away to nothing. I couldn't imagine where it was going. In all the weeks we'd been at the cabin, I'd never even noticed a beaver lodge. Where was this guy — or gal — from? Was it going to the same place the mink had gone?

Alice was right: there was so much we didn't know.

I looked up toward the darkened woods. How much life was packed into just one of those towering trees? Beetles, squirrels, woodpeckers, ants, bees, eagles: there they were, day in and day out, burrowing and perching, hatching and dying. A whole world on a stem. And what was creeping on the ground under the fallen leaves and pine needles? What was boring through the dirt? What was hiding within all those impenetrable shrubs?

It was strange how little we thought about any of that stuff.

Every summer, we came to the cabin and settled into our routines. We talked about *our* woods and *our* lake, creating our memories. But what about all these other animals? Wasn't it their woods and their lake — even more than ours? It made me wonder how the world of Three Bird Lake looked through their eyes. Was it safe or precarious? Were we humans terrible intruders or uninteresting lumps? Did they think of the lake as quiet, like we did? Or did they think it was loud with all of us here? Did they hate our smells?

I looked around me again at the water and the shore, wondering what sorts of invisible paths and posts the mink and beavers and deer and rabbits had here. We glimpsed only the temporary traces, like when the mink left their footsteps in the mud or the deer left their droppings in the woods. Did the animals here — like that beaver I'd seen tonight — have maps inside their heads, with routes to food and friends and safe havens?

And then I knew. All of a sudden I understood the puzzle of Grandma's treasure map. The mysterious G had left us a huge clue, and we'd been too focused on our own dumb selves to notice it.

I was so excited, I felt like screaming across the water for Alice to come out. We could find the treasure now — I was sure of it! How could I wait an entire night to tell her?

I settled for jumping up and down on the dock and waving my hands in the air as the stars came popping out — little pinpricks in a giant black balloon. I was glad there was no one to witness my little celebration except maybe a bat or two. But I felt more excited than I had in a long time, and nothing could keep me from showing it.

27

IN THE MORNING, Mom went to pick up Grandma from the hospital. As soon as she was gone, I rode my bike over to Alice's house. I was so excited to share my discovery about the treasure map with her that I almost forgot what a jerk I'd been the last time we spoke. But clearly Alice hadn't forgotten.

Mrs. Jensen answered the door and went to find Alice, only to return looking flustered.

"I'm sorry, Adam," she said. "Alice isn't feeling well this morning."

"Oh," I said. I felt myself blushing slightly, wondering if Mrs. Jensen knew what was going on.

"If she feels better later, would you have her give me a call?" I asked.

Mrs. Jensen nodded. "Will your grandmother be coming home soon?" she asked gently.

"Today," I told her. "My mom just went to get her."

"Well, that's good," Mrs. Jensen went on. "I'm sure your grandmother will be very glad to see you when she gets home."

That felt like my cue to leave. I said good-bye and headed over to where I'd left my bike. As I passed a corner window, I caught sight of someone peering through the glass, but then she ducked out of sight behind a white lacy curtain. I sighed. It had to be Alice.

I rode back home. As soon as I was back at the empty cabin, I regretted my hasty return. I couldn't stay here alone. I couldn't stand around not looking for the treasure. And I couldn't look for the treasure without Alice. We were a team.

I found paper and a pen in the house and scrawled her a note. It took some thought. In the end, I wrote,

Hey, Alice,
Three things:
1. I'm sorry.
2. I think I know how we can find the treasure!
    Please come over.

3. *I really am sorry.*
— *Adam*

I folded the note into quarters. This time I didn't bother with the bike; I cut into the woods and did my best to follow Poison Ivy Parkway all the way to Alice's house. When I emerged into her clearing, I paused. Should I give the note to her mom? That was a little too embarrassing. But how else to get it to Alice? I had a pretty good sense of which window belonged to Alice's room now, and I slowly made my way toward it, hoping I wouldn't be spotted by Mr. or Mrs. Jensen. Once there, I wedged the note into a corner of the screen, knocked hard on the glass of the window above, and then sprinted back to the edge of the woods, waiting and watching.

Moments later, I saw the screen slide open, and Alice's hand grabbed hold of the note. I hung around for a few minutes, waiting to see if she'd come outside, but eventually I gave up. I turned and made my way toward home, wondering if I'd said enough to convince her to come out.

Just as I reached our drive, I heard footsteps crashing behind me.

"Hey!" Alice said when she reached my side. Her cheeks were flushed, and her shoelaces weren't even tied.

"Hi," I said. "Are you feeling better?"

She looked me in the eye and nodded. "Nothing like a good apology or two to heal that kind of malady."

"I was being kind of ridiculous," I told her. "Can you just forget everything I said?"

"That's a funny request, coming from Memory Guy," she said with a smile. "But OK."

We kept walking, climbing the steps onto the deck and sitting on the built-in seats facing each other.

"I should have told you about the tennis," Alice said. "And about meeting up with Drew. Here's all of it, OK? I'm captain of my middle-school tennis team, and I was a three-time age-group champion in my old league. I like playing tennis. But I still don't hang out with the popular girls and I did go to Camp Watson and you saw my mutant toes." She made a goofy face. "So I wasn't lying about all that."

"I know, Duck," I said, smiling.

"Good. Now, are you going to tell me about the map, or what?"

"We were measuring wrong," I told her.

"What do you mean?" she asked. "We tried the whole thing with my steps and your steps and a tall Minnesotan's steps!"

"I know," I said. "But we didn't try animal steps."

"Animal steps?"

"Think about it," I said. "Every path has a different

209

animal name. So if it's Hare Highway, shouldn't you measure the distance in rabbit steps? And measure Deer Drive in deer steps? And Beaver Boulevard in beaver steps?"

"I guess you could," Alice said. "But how do you know for sure?"

"Well, I don't," I admitted. I'd been more sure of myself the night before, alone under the stars. "But it just fits somehow. I think it's worth a try."

"Of course we'll try. It has potential, actually," Alice said. Her eyes fairly flashed as she took in my information. "There will be so much variation, won't there? We're going to end up in a totally different place!"

I nodded.

"How'd you think of this, anyway?" she asked.

I told her about seeing the beaver the night before and about thinking of the animals and the different paths they took. The final piece was when I was remembering the mink we'd seen and picturing the tracks they'd left behind.

Alice smiled. "Good thing I'm working with Memory Guy here. I never would have remembered mink footprints!" She jumped up. "So come on! What are we waiting for?"

The sound of a car in the drive made us look up. It was my mom, with my grandmother in the passenger seat. I couldn't help feeling disappointed, even though I knew it was selfish of me.

"Oh," I said to Alice. "I don't think I can leave right now."

"Right," she said.

"But my grandmother usually naps after lunch. Can you come over then?"

"Sure," she said. "I just hope I can stand waiting that long!"

I nodded sympathetically. "You still have the map?" I asked.

"Of course," she said.

She skipped down the steps and, with a quick wave to my mom and grandma, bolted into the woods for home.

Mom got out of the car and strode deliberately over to the passenger side, but Grandma had already opened the door and was getting out on her own. Mom made a gesture of helping, but Grandma was back on her land and was having none of it. She pushed Mom lightly out of her way, then looked up into the tops of the trees. It was then I saw the white bandage across her forehead and a dark line under one eye.

"Welcome back, Grandma," I said as I drew near.

"I hear you had a nice night by yourself," she said. Her voice was dry and a little slow, but I could tell she was determined to sound strong. "I hope you didn't have a wild party."

"It was wild enough without a party," I said. "How are you doing?"

She rolled her eyes, pointing to the bandage and to a piece of tape folded over her glasses. "I need new spectacles. Possibly a new head. Otherwise, I'm aces."

"Adam, can you bring in the things from the back of the car? I'll help Grandma inside," Mom said.

Grandma shook her head. "I can walk just fine," she said. "It's cars that give me trouble."

I stole a glance at Mom. For once, she let the comment go.

"Well, let's go in together anyway," she said. "I think we could all do with some lunch."

Grandma followed her up the steps and into the house. She looked shrunken and less steady than before. But having her back in the cabin felt right, like when you snap a missing jigsaw puzzle piece into place. I'm sure she felt the same way.

28

WE HAD LUNCH TOGETHER, Grandma and I sitting at the table while Mom buzzed around us with the fixings. When Mom finally sat down, we settled into awkward small talk. No one seemed ready or willing to talk about serious matters.

"How was the hospital food, Grandma?" I asked.

She shook her head. "Cardboard and cotton balls. It was junk when I was a nurse. And it's even worse now. Did you see the color of that Jell-O?"

"We're glad you didn't have to stay in for long," Mom said.

Grandma grunted in agreement.

"Yeah, you wouldn't want to miss more than a day of pancakes," I pointed out. I caught Mom's eye, but she was too preoccupied to remember our joke from the day before.

Mom grew restless as soon as her plate was empty. I knew that she was stewing over what to do with Grandma — whether we could squeeze an extra day or two into our visit, and how to get Grandma back to St. Paul before we drove home.

"In case you were wondering," Grandma said when she was done eating, "I'm not leaving till October."

Mom attempted a supportive nod.

"And now I'm going to go take a nap," Grandma announced, standing up. "Don't let your mother make any plans while I'm asleep. It's not respectful."

"OK, Grandma," I said.

I was outside swinging on the hammock when Alice appeared, carrying a small stack of papers.

"You're not sleeping, are you?" she asked.

"Are you kidding?" I swung my feet off the hammock, ready to start our search.

"I have the map," Alice said when she was close enough to talk quietly. "And I also did a little research while I was home."

"Research?" I asked.

"I figured we probably don't know as much as G and your grandma did about animals and their tracks. So I got some good information."

"Smart," I said.

"It's actually really interesting," she said. "So you start with their step length — which some people call their stride. Apparently you measure it from the back of one foot to the back of the next." She demonstrated with her own stride.

"OK. That makes sense," I said.

"But there are all these crazy variables. Are they walking or bounding or galloping? There's this huge range in step lengths to cover all the different ways the animal might move."

I frowned. "So what numbers do we use?"

"I'm guessing we can just go with averages. I mean, G was probably estimating when he made the map . . . assuming he was even using animal paces in the first place."

"Well, it's worth a try," I said, trying to regain some of my earlier optimism.

We started at the back corner of the cabin again and used measuring tape that Alice had brought to count off paces. Our first direction was to take fifty steps on Mouse Main Street. When we'd done this before, we'd ended up well into the woods, but now we barely got out of the shadow of the cabin. We followed Chipmunk Chute and Beaver Boulevard, and when we angled toward the lake on Mink Meander, we didn't even come close to getting our feet wet in the lake.

"It feels more right, doesn't it?" Alice said, her voice scarcely containing her excitement.

"It's definitely drier!"

Two hundred paces on Deer Drive took us up well past the cabin again — a deer's walking stride turned out to be pretty close to our own. But by the time we finished all the other parts of our walk, we weren't very deep in the woods at all. Instead, we were just beyond the grassy clearing where my mom had pitched her tent as a kid. There were lots of trees — birches and pines and spruces and oaks — surrounded by bushes that grew so thick they could have concealed a good-size piano. In summers past, my cousins and I had lost tons of baseballs in these woods, even after we thought we'd seen where they had fallen. If the treasure was in here somewhere, it was going to take an excellent system or good luck to find it. Probably both.

"Let's try to cover this whole area," I said to Alice, gesturing in a wide circle around us. "Remember, we were estimating those animal paces. We haven't pinpointed anything yet."

"Right-o," Alice said. "I'll start with these shrubby

things and work my way over to there," she said, pointing off in the direction of her property.

"And I'll start with that big pine tree," I said, pointing to the tallest one in sight. I walked over slowly, keeping my eyes focused on the ground so I wouldn't miss a single clue. I had to believe that G would have made it fairly obvious if he'd buried the treasure. Maybe he would have piled up rocks to make a cairn on top of it. Or drawn that target symbol. Once I reached the tree, I circled its trunk, then looked up into the canopy for something stowed up high. I even pulled myself up into the lower branches in case G was a climber, but all I got for my effort was a lot of sap on my hands.

Alice peeked behind a section of peeled birch bark. "Maybe he wrote her a message on birch bark," she called.

"Or carved their initials," I suggested.

Several minutes later, Alice gave a little shout of discovery.

"What?" I asked, jogging over. "Did you find something?"

Alice was leaning into a dense patch of blueberries. "Ta-da!" she said, pulling out a white plastic Frisbee now covered with grass stains and dirt.

"Ha!" I said. "I think that used to belong to my cousins."

"Let me guess," Alice said. "They were playing lake Frisbee?"

"Actually, I think they were trying to knock a bee-hive out of a tree," I said.

"Such smart boys," Alice said, shaking her head. "Come on — let's get back to work."

I continued searching my area, trying to be as thorough as possible. I peered into shrubs, fingered every tree trunk, and kicked away the leaves and sticks on the forest floor in case they covered a hole or a marker. When I'd finally finished, I looked over at Alice. She was on her hands and knees, crawling through the grasses and ferns like a crazed badger snuffling out its next meal. "You almost done?" I asked.

"I'm not even halfway!" she said. She looked up, tucking a strand of hair behind her ear. "You went too fast."

"I'm just really efficient," I insisted. "I can come over there and help, if you want."

Alice shook her head and went back to her ground search. "That's OK," she said. "I've got a system here."

I was never going to be able to match Alice's attention to detail, and I couldn't very well hurry her along. So I sat down and leaned against a tree to wait. It was nice here in the woods, with the leaves and the bark and the berries. Especially now that the mosquitoes had mostly scattered. I spun the old Frisbee in my hands and inhaled the sweet air. Maybe this was treasure enough.

Meanwhile, Alice kept busy. She inspected, dug, climbed, peered, and scanned. All she needed was a magnifying glass and a clipboard, and she'd look like a professional scientist.

I stopped spinning the Frisbee and gazed for a moment at its surface. "Wait," I said to Alice. "What if this isn't my cousins' Frisbee?"

"What?" Alice asked.

"It would be the perfect thing to mark G's treasure. Look at it — it looks just like a target. See the concentric rings? Maybe he buried the treasure under this."

"It doesn't look that old," Alice said, coming over for a closer look. "Besides, did they even have plastic Frisbees back then?"

"Nah, I guess not," I said, spinning the Frisbee some more. "Not like this one, anyway."

Alice scratched her head. "But actually, there *is* something out here with concentric rings. I mean, besides the Frisbee."

"What?" I asked.

"Trees!" she said. "You know, round trunks, rings inside. Kind of like a target symbol!"

We gazed around us at all the tree trunks in sight. There must have been twenty, thirty trees within our view. For a moment, I could almost sense the trees laughing at us.

"Should we dig under every one?" Alice asked.

"Maybe," I said. "But we don't even know if we're in the right place. I'm starting to think this whole search might be kind of crazy."

"Oh, I don't mind," Alice said. "Crazy's fun!"

The truth is, Alice could make anything fun. "Crazy's fine," I said. "But if we're going to start excavating the entire woods, I'm going to need a snack."

"Mom's making cinnamon buns," Alice said, raising her eyebrows.

"Yum," I said.

"First one there gets two," she taunted.

She took off running in the direction of her cabin. I leaped to my feet and raced after her at top speed. But before I'd gone ten steps, my foot caught on a raised tree root and I pitched forward, falling to the ground. Alice came jogging back, gushing apologies.

"Oh, gosh, Adam, I'm so sorry," she said, coming to kneel beside me. "Are you OK?"

I rubbed my knees and brushed a trickle of blood from my dirt-covered hand. "I'm OK," I said, feeling completely stupid.

"Oh, my gosh!" Alice repeated.

"It's just a scratch," I said, holding up my palm. "See?"

But Alice wasn't paying attention to me at all. Instead, she was staring at an enormous tree stump beside us. "Look!" she said.

Tall grasses had grown up around most of the stump, but eventually I noticed what Alice had seen — a piece of wood that didn't match the bark beside it. I leaned forward and parted the grasses.

Someone had placed a piece of cut wood over part of the stump. On the right side of the wood was an ancient metal thumbtack, stuck into the wood like a doorknob. We stared in stunned silence. There was only one thing this could be.

"Oh. My. God," Alice said. "I can't breathe."

"This is it," I said. "It is, isn't it?" My voice was shaky.

Alice nodded. "Open it," she whispered.

I reached forward and tugged on the pushpin. Nothing happened.

"Here, hand me the measuring tape," I said to Alice.

She handed me the tape and I used the metal end to trace the seams of the door. I pulled again. This time it opened — on tiny metal hinges.

"Whoa!" Alice said.

Behind the door was a natural hollow where the wood had rotted away. It was dark and full of tree debris, but we could see the edge of a square metal box lying inside.

"This is so intense!" Alice said, gripping my knee.

"Should I . . . ?" I asked, gesturing inside.

Alice nodded. I reached my hand inside and pulled out the box.

We stared in wonder at its top.

"For Viola. Forever," Alice read.

The words were written on the surface in black paint. They had lasted for more than half a century. Now all we had to do was lift the cover to find the treasure hidden inside.

"Should we take it to her right away?" Alice said.

"Before we look inside?" I asked. It hadn't occurred to me for a moment that we wouldn't get the first look. But I had to admit that Alice had a point. "It's hers, really, isn't it?"

"On the other hand," Alice went on, thinking it through, "I guess we don't know if whatever he gave her is still, you know, presentable."

"Right. It could be moldy cookies, decayed flowers," I said. "We'd better check it out. Just in case."

Alice nodded, and I slowly lifted the lid. Lying inside was a cloth bag tied with string. I loosened the ties and stretched the opening wide, peering in.

"Oh," I said.

"What is it? What is it?" Alice asked.

"It's not moldy cookies," I told her.

I reached into the bag and pulled out a small wooden loon, expertly carved. Its beak was pointing up, as if it was just finishing a gulp of water. Lines of feathers defined a simple wing.

"Look at that!" Alice exclaimed. "It's gorgeous!"

But there was more. Next I pulled out a squat beaver. Then a deer. Then a bear.

"These are amazing!" Alice said. "And to think, no one has touched them in decades! I'm getting goose bumps!"

There were seven animals in all. Alice picked them up one by one, turning them over and rubbing their smooth sides.

"He sure had a thing for animals," I said.

"And what an artist," Alice said. Then she gasped. "You know . . ." An enormous grin spread across her face. "I think I just figured out who G is!" She drummed her thighs with excitement. "Do you know?"

I shook my head. "Is he some famous sculptor or something?"

"Nope," Alice said a little smugly. "Don't these look a little bit familiar to you somehow?" she hinted.

They did, actually, but I had no idea why. And I didn't appreciate it when Alice burst into laughter. "Think, Adam! Think!!"

"What?" I asked, still not getting it.

"The mantel . . . Those little carved spaces. These are the same animals!"

I looked at the animals again. Of course: bear, loon, beaver, fish, squirrel, wolf, and deer. They were the same seven animals on the mantel in Grandma's living room.

"Alice," I said, "do you think they fit into those spaces?"

"I bet they do," she said. "It's like he carved the outline of the animal for the mantel, and then turned the leftover piece of wood into a three-dimensional figure."

I saw it all now, just as Alice did. "So G is the builder's son!"

"It sure looks like that to me," Alice said. "Do you know his name?"

I shook my head. "Not yet," I said. I picked up the animals again, one by one, imagining the hands that carved them into life.

"This whole thing is so amazing," Alice said. She opened and closed the little wooden door, then examined the whole tree stump, brushing off the dirt and needles that had piled up on top. "And here's our target," she added, pointing out the tree rings.

I shook my head in amazement. Frustrated as we'd been in certain moments, we'd actually been working with one super tightly constructed treasure map.

I looked at the animals in my lap. "I've got to show

these to her," I said. "But I don't want my mom around. She doesn't even know about G. And she obviously knows nothing about the treasure."

"Can you wait till she's out of the house or something?"

I shook my head. "How? She's in full-time planning mode about how to get Grandma packed up and out of here. And I don't think I can invent any old errand to distract her." I put the animals back in the bag, then settled it into the metal box.

Alice watched me, looking thoughtful. "I know what to do," she said after a few moments. "Just leave it to me."

29

WHEN ALICE AND I got back to the cabin, Grandma was still in her room and Mom was taking a shower. We pulled one of the animals from the bag — the bear — and slid it into its space on the carved mantel. It was a perfect fit.

Alice gave me a thumbs-up sign, and we put the bear back in the bag.

"I'd better go now," she whispered. "Stick around. If this works like I want it to, your mom will be getting a phone call in about fifteen minutes."

I felt suddenly uncomfortable. "This isn't a mean trick, is it?" I asked.

Alice frowned. "When are you going to finally believe that I'm a nice person?" she asked.

"I'm sorry," I said. "That was a dumb thing to say."

I hid the treasure box under my bed and waited to hear Mom come out of the shower and go into her room. A few minutes later she emerged, dressed and ready, it seemed, for action. She had a pen behind her ear and a thick notepad in her hands. She passed me sitting on the couch pretending to read a book.

"It's not fair of Grandma to tell me not to make plans," she said.

"Have you talked to Uncle Martin?" I asked.

"He said he could come stay for the week after we go," she said. "But that hardly seems worth it."

I shrugged. "She'll appreciate every day."

Then, right on schedule, the phone rang. I heard Mom talking to Mrs. Jensen for a few minutes about Grandma, and then, to my surprise, she ended by saying, "Why, that would be lovely, thank you. I'll see you in a few minutes!"

"Are you going out?" I asked her.

She nodded. "Mrs. Jensen offered to help me strategize," she said, sounding amazed. "I'll have a quick cup of tea over there and be right back." She picked up her purse and her calendar. "What's the fastest way?"

"You can try Poison Ivy Parkway," I said.

Mom looked at me with confusion.

"Maybe you should drive," I said.

She nodded and left.

I was growing impatient waiting for Grandma to wake up. She never took such long naps. Was it because of the stroke? The hospital stay? For a brief moment, I had the morbid thought that maybe she'd died in her sleep, so I was doubly relieved when I heard a sound in her room moments later. I peeked in through a crack in the doorway. She was sitting up in bed, and when I knocked and opened the door, I realized she'd been awake for some time. There were papers surrounding her on the bed, and she was reading.

"Hi, Grandma," I said, hoping like crazy that she was going to be clear-headed now, not lost in the past as she'd been the last time I'd seen her looking at old papers.

"Hi, Adam," she said. "Did I hear your mother go out?"

"Yeah. She just went next door."

"Good," she said. "I'd like to take a walk down to the lake and say hello. Before your mother tells me it's time to say good-bye."

She started stacking up the papers, but before she was done, I sat down beside her.

"Grandma, can we talk?" I asked her.

She eyed me uncertainly. "What for?"

I looked down at my feet and tried to think of what to say next.

"Is this about my accident?" she asked.

"No, not that. It's about . . ." My voice trailed off. I almost said "G," but that seemed too obscure. "It's about, um, the treasure."

"Treasure?" she asked, looking at me blankly.

I realized I didn't even know how to start. I took a deep breath. "Grandma, before your accident, you wrote me notes. You left them in my room. Do you remember?"

Grandma frowned and shook her head. "I don't know what you're talking about."

I forged on. "Notes. Kind of . . . personal ones," I said, trying not to blush. "You wrote them to someone named G, and you talked about missing him and about a treasure he'd left for you. . . ."

Grandma's gray eyebrows gathered together like mini storm clouds. "Stop right there, Adam! What have you been doing? Going through my personal things? I didn't know you were the kind of kid who did such . . . such . . ."

"Grandma, please!" I interrupted. My voice cracked. I never imagined she'd be angry at me. It was true, I guess — I *had* gone through her things when I'd taken the map. But she didn't even know about that yet.

"You really did write me notes," I said. "I'm telling the truth! You left them in my room when you were . . . confused. Like the way you were at the hospital."

At the mention of the hospital, she grew quiet. She looked at me apprehensively and took a small breath. "What did they say?"

"Nothing much," I told her. "They were hard to follow. But I figured out, I mean, I think I figured out there was somebody before my grandfather. Somebody whose name started with G."

"Gil," my grandmother said, almost in a whisper.

"Was he the builder's son? The one who carved the mantel and the porch rail?" I asked.

She nodded.

"He was an artist," I said.

She nodded again. "He was a lovely boy."

When I looked at her face then, full of its lines and creases, I thought how an old person's face was almost its own kind of map. Trails of joy, furrows of anger, lines of sadness — it was all there for a person to read. But it could also change. Looking at her now, the anger wasn't so visible; instead, I saw all the sadness and hurt in sloping trails beside her eyes.

"You really liked him, didn't you?" I said, surprising myself when the words came out. Maybe I wanted to hear more of the happy part of the story, because I already knew it didn't end the way Grandma had wanted.

Grandma sighed. "We met when he was helping his father build the house. We were just teenagers, you know. But back then, sixteen or seventeen wasn't too early to talk about marriage. My dad was very critical of Gil, though. Said he was too much of a daydreamer. A romantic. So I kept our relationship a secret. Everyone thought we were just friends."

"Even Dottie?" I asked.

"She hardly knew him. She was away working as a camp counselor that first summer," Grandma said. "The following June, we were all back at the lake. I was just getting ready to tell her about Gil when she introduced me to your grandfather. And then . . ." She trailed off.

I didn't say anything, just waited and watched. Grandma really was a tough old bird—she still didn't cry as she told me about the accident. Gil had been driving his truck back to his house one afternoon when he lost control and drove off the road over an embankment. The truck flipped and he'd been terribly hurt. He lasted one day in the hospital before dying, but Grandma had never seen him again.

"He was conscious when they first brought him to the hospital," she said quietly. "He told them he swerved so he wouldn't hit a butterfly." She smiled ruefully and shook her head.

I pictured the moment: the delicate butterfly, the heavy metal truck.

"That was Gil for you," Grandma said. "He was so talented. And so smart. But he was almost too sweet for his own good, and he had a huge soft spot for animals."

I wanted to hear more about him, but it didn't seem like the time. "I'm sorry, Grandma," I said instead.

"Well, don't be too sorry," she said, recovering her usual voice. "If I hadn't married your grandfather, you wouldn't be sitting here today!"

I could tell that she was ready to be done talking, but I still hadn't told her about the box. "Grandma," I said, "I found Gil's treasure map that day you asked me to file some papers. You'd mentioned it in one of your notes."

I waited for her to erupt, but she only scowled. "That old thing? Gil gave me that a few days before the accident. He thought it would be fun to send me off running through the woods on a wild-goose chase. And of course at first I thought it was great sport. Then Gil was gone and that map became a torment! That boy was a wonderful artist, but he didn't have the least idea how to make a map. I tried it hundreds of times. But I never found anything at the end of my route."

I looked at Grandma, unable to contain a smile.

"What?" she said.

"We found it," I said.

"We?"

"Alice and me," I said. "We found the treasure, Grandma. We found it this morning!"

Her eyes widened behind her glasses, and her expression was almost like a child's again. "You have it?" she whispered.

I nodded.

"Here?"

"It's in my room," I said.

"Well, then, what are you waiting for? Go get it!" she said.

I hurried out of the room and came back with the box. There was still dirt on the bottom, but I knew Grandma wouldn't care. I placed it on top of the quilt covering her lap.

She traced a shaky finger over the inscription. *For Viola. Forever.* A tear slipped down her cheek, and then another. Feeling suddenly awkward, I started to get up to give her some privacy. But she laid a hand on my knee.

"Stay," she said.

She placed both hands back on the box. Wizened and spotted, thin and frail — they weren't the hands that were supposed to be doing this. They were supposed to be young hands. Teenage hands.

Grandma gingerly lifted the cover off the box and set it aside. She stared for a moment at the little cloth bag. Then she took it in her hands, pulled it open, and slipped her hand inside. She felt around with her eyes closed for several seconds, then spilled all the animals onto her lap.

"Oh," she said with a hushed gasp. "You see. . . ." Her voice trailed off. She picked up the bear and gently stroked it head to tail as if smoothing its shaggy fur. Then she slid it between the pinkie and ring finger of her left hand and held it there. She picked up the loon, turning it left and right, and then slid it between the next two fingers, beside the bear. She admired and caressed each animal in turn — even the fat fish — and placed them between her fingers until all seven were upright in her two hands. Then she held them out in front of her, not able — or maybe just not bothering — to wipe away the tears that had come now, like rain on cracked earth. She drew the animals to her face and kissed them, with a quiet sob. "It almost feels as if he's here again," she said. "Oh, sweet Gil."

After a few minutes, she set the animals down and took off her glasses. I handed her a tissue, and she wiped her eyes.

"Well," she said. She looked at me with an expression that said "I guess you've seen it all now."

"They're amazing, aren't they?" I said. "And they fit. In the mantel. You probably already figured that out."

Grandma nodded. "That's what I guessed. How on earth did you find this, Adam? I tried that map so many times."

"Remember the paces?" I said. "Two hundred paces on Deer Drive, thirty paces on Beaver Boulevard . . . that kind of thing?"

She nodded.

"You had to measure animal steps — you know, the deer's and the beaver's steps. Not human steps."

"Animal steps," Grandma said, shaking her head. "Oh, that is just like Gil. Why didn't I think of that in all these years?"

"I'm still not sure we would have found it, though, if we hadn't, er, kind of stumbled across it," I admitted. I told her about the tree stump and the little door, and promised to take her there as soon as she felt up for a walk in the woods again.

"Well, thank you. To you and Alice both."

I smiled, then stood up from the bed. Grandma put her glasses back on. She picked up the animals again. "No word about any of this to your mother, right?"

I started to agree, then hesitated. "Maybe you should just tell her, Grandma."

"Tell her?"

It was something I couldn't quite put into words, so I just said, "It might help her. Knowing more."

"I'll take that into consideration," Grandma said, but not fiercely.

As I headed out the door, she called me back. "Say, Adam?"

I stopped and looked at her expectantly.

"I truly loved my Gil," she said. "But I'm glad I married your grandfather. We had some very good years together. And best of all, he gave me your mother and your uncle Martin. And he gave me you."

"Thanks," I said.

"You're a treasure, too, you know," she fairly whispered.

"Thanks," I said again, then left her to her thoughts.

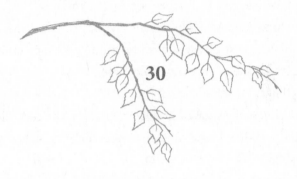

30

WHEN MOM CAME BACK from visiting with Mrs. Jensen, Grandma was sitting on the dock, wrapped up in a dark wool shirt that had belonged to my grandfather. She looked as tough and old as always, but for the first time ever I felt like I was looking at her all the way through, seeing or at least sensing her inner depths. Being old had to be so strange — to know you looked ragged on the outside, but to still feel inside, at least sometimes, like the fresh young person you once were.

Mom walked up the steps and put her arms around me, taking me by surprise. I think I flinched, but she didn't let go and I relaxed into her hold. We watched

Grandma together then, in silence. When she finally let go, I turned to look at her and was surprised to see her beaming.

"Did something good happen?" I asked.

"Betty — Mrs. Jensen — is a wonderful person."

"Did she give you cinnamon rolls?" I asked.

Mom laughed. "You're a funny kid, Adam. I mean that in the best of ways. No, she didn't give me cinnamon rolls. She made everything better."

"How?"

"I knew she worked in hospice back in Minneapolis. What I didn't know was that she's an instructor in nursing."

"How does that help?"

"When she heard about our problem with Grandma, she had a wonderful idea. It seems there's a student of hers — a young woman named Carrie — who's had to take a break from the program because she just had a baby. She's a single mom, and money is tight. So Betty suggested we contact her to see if she would stay with Grandma."

"You mean, you'll hire her to be Grandma's nurse?" I asked.

"Not hire. We couldn't afford to hire a full-time nurse, and Grandma would object if we did anyway. This is more like a trade that allows everyone to hold on to their pride. Carrie will live with Grandma and keep an eye on her in exchange for a free place to live and a hand with the baby."

"Will they live here? Or in St. Paul?" I asked, still trying to see how this could all work.

"Both," my mom said. "Carrie can live anywhere until January, when she reenters her program. And then St. Paul is perfect. She can commute to school from Grandma's place."

This was starting to sound too good to be true. "What if Carrie doesn't want to live with an old lady as cranky as Grandma?" I asked.

"We already called her," Mom said, her voice thick with relief and joy. "And she said yes!"

I was amazed. Here I'd thought Alice was going to make up a silly trick to lure my mom out of the house, and instead she and her mom had found a way to solve my family's biggest problem. She really was a genius. Or maybe just one of the nicest people I'd ever met.

"So when are you going to talk to Grandma about this?" I asked Mom. The whole time we'd been talking, Grandma hadn't moved from her spot on the dock. If she heard Mom's car — or even our distant voices — she wasn't letting on.

Mom looked down toward the dock. "I think now would be perfect," she said. She squeezed my arms again and then headed for the path. She didn't walk in her usual fast and purposeful way; instead, she worked her way slowly down the slope, radiating relief.

I stayed long enough to see Grandma turn her head in Mom's direction and to see them start talking. I didn't want to watch the conversation unfold. I wasn't sure why — maybe it felt like spying, or maybe I just wanted to cut to the end and know that everything had worked out OK. For both of them.

When I went back into the cabin, I saw that Grandma had set each of the carved animals into its spot in the mantel. They looked beautiful that way — filling in what had once been just outline and empty space with their woody weight, exactly where they belonged.

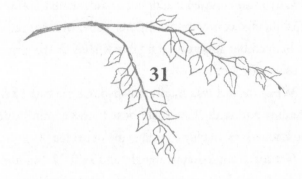

31

ON OUR LAST NIGHT at the cabin, we had a feast. An old-fashioned crowd-around-the-table feast like we hadn't had since the cabin was stuffed with cousins. Uncle Martin had driven up with Carrie and her baby. Mom had invited Dottie Lewis and her daughter, and the Jensens, including, of course, Alice.

The eleven of us crowded around the long kitchen table and ate grilled walleye, biscuits, corn on the cob, salad, and three kinds of pie. Mom's cheeks were pink — from the cooking or a rare glass of wine, it was hard to tell which — and she looked completely at ease. Dottie kept everyone laughing, including Grandma, and Mr. Jensen proved to be a pretty good storyteller, although Alice and I exchanged pained glances when he started spinning a story about the day we disappeared into the Minnesota wilderness.

Carrie didn't say a lot at first, but she seemed to enjoy the exuberant company. So did her baby, who squealed and banged her spoon on the table whenever the group got especially loud.

When dessert was finally finished, Carrie turned to Grandma and said, "I don't suppose there's anyone here who knows how to play a good game of bridge."

Grandma smiled approvingly and said, "We nurses will be a team." Soon a card table was set up in front of the fire, with Grandma and Carrie taking on Uncle Martin and Mr. Jensen. Dottie, her daughter, Mom, and Mrs. Jensen plopped down on the couches and continued the dinnertime chatter as they took turns passing Carrie's baby from lap to lap.

It was a lot of ladies and a whole lot of girl talk, but I hardly noticed.

Alice and I were washing the dishes together at the kitchen sink, shoulder to shoulder. It was like we were in our own separate space. Alice scrubbed the dishes in the soapy tub, then dunked them in the big basin of steaming rinse water. I dried and stacked.

"I love what your grandmother did with the animals," Alice said.

"Me, too," I told her. The mantel had never looked incomplete before, but now it looked alive, inhabited.

"Did you see her take me aside?" Alice asked. "She thanked me for helping find them. And she said the best part was that she now had a little part of the cabin she could take back to the city with her."

"I like that," I said. But the mention of the word "city" made my heart sink.

"We'll all be back here before we know it, of course," Alice said, as if reading my mind.

I shrugged. Next June felt like a long way away to me.

When Dottie and her daughter announced that it was time to go, the Jensens said they ought to be heading home, too, and everyone made for the door. Mom and I were leaving at the crack of dawn the next morning, so these were our final farewells. I was disappointed that I'd have to say good-bye to Alice in front of all the grown-ups, but there didn't seem to be any way around it. Then Mom asked the Jensens if Alice could stay a little longer and help me watch the baby while she and Carrie made up the guest beds, promising that we'd be sure to get Alice home safely. She said it so naturally that not a single grown-up chuckled, not even Grandma. But

I knew she was thinking about me, because when the beds were done, she handed me a flashlight, saying, "I wouldn't want to walk on Poison Ivy Parkway even if I *could* find it. You go!"

"Sure," I said. I think she knew how grateful I was.

It was the first time Alice and I had ever been out in the woods in the inky Minnesota dark. The air was cool and fragrant. Insects clattered around us. The world felt bigger and more full of possibility.

"Do you think we can find the path?" I asked Alice.

"Sure," she said. "Follow me."

We pushed our way through the branches and brush, following the small circle of light from the flashlight.

"I wonder where our mink are right now," Alice said.

I smiled at the thought of them as ours, but I didn't have an answer.

It was the perfect August night. It felt like we should have been embarking on a new adventure — staying up all night, starting a week-long camping trip — not bringing summer to an end. All too soon, I spotted the Jensens' porch light in the distance.

"Here we are," Alice said.

"Yep," I said.

We stood tentatively on the edge of the woods. Across Alice's yard, fireflies punctuated the darkness with their secret signals.

"So will you guys be back again next summer?" Alice asked me.

"Of course," I said. "How about you?"

"Yeah. I'm definitely done with Geek Camp. This place is a lot more fun." She hesitated and then looked up at me. In the faint illumination of the flashlight, I could see a slightly impish smile on her face. "Do you think, next summer when we're thirteen . . . do you think maybe then you'll be ready to kiss me?"

I was glad it was too dark for her to see my red ears. "Maybe," I said.

"I mean, if you're not still dating Grandma!" she added.

"Yeah, yeah," I said, grateful to have her break the tension. Then I remembered something. "Oh, hey, I have something for you." I reached into the pocket of my sweatshirt and brought out the rubber crayfish I'd bought at Thompson's Dime Store. I wiggled it in front of the flashlight, making its pinchers sway back and forth like the moves of a really bad dancer. Alice burst out laughing.

I put it into her hands. "Maybe it'll help you on those bad days at school."

"How could it not?" Alice said, giving it another shake. "When the going gets tough, the tough dance like crazed crayfish!"

"Exactly."

"Thanks. It's awesome. Really." She glanced toward the house. "I guess I'd better go, then," she said, turning away. "So, bye."

"Bye, Duck," I said with a slight wave. I took a step toward the woods but then stopped. "Wait."

"Yeah?" she asked.

"I was just thinking," I said, walking back toward her. "I'm Memory Guy. I mean, he's a superhero. He's the kind of fellow who saves the world and then gets the —" My voice caught.

"Girl?" Alice asked hopefully.

"Yeah," I said. I took another step to close the distance between us and leaned forward. She smelled like wood smoke and cherry pie and the Minnesota night. I planted a kiss on her lips. Just like that.

It was absolutely electrifying.

I think Alice felt it, too. She grinned so broadly, she practically made her own light.

"See you next summer, then," she said.

"Definitely," I told her.

I stepped into the woods, turned off the flashlight, and bounded home.

ACKNOWLEDGMENTS

A book such as this one incorporates a lifetime of experiences and influences, more than I can possibly cite. I do want to acknowledge my paddling partners: my childhood friends in Ann Arbor, John and Anne Knott, and the intrepid Cone-Miller clan. Four teachers — Lois Theis, Phil Rusten, Helen Hill, and Jim Shepard — nurtured important parts of this storytelling. The Robert and Patricia Switzer Foundation and its network supported every turn in my professional path with uncommon broad-mindedness and trust. Blyth Lord never stopped believing. I thank my wonderful editor, Kaylan Adair, for taking on a quiet novel at a time when quietness is often in short supply. I thank my family members — *todos santos* — especially Addie and Margot, my wondrous readers, and Robin, my everything. Most of all I acknowledge my mother, Lloyd, the first and most loyal supporter of my writing, who I wish with all my heart were here now to hold this book in her hands.

SARA ST. ANTOINE was eight years old when she first paddled a canoe — on the Huron River in her hometown of Ann Arbor, Michigan. Within moments, she struck an overhanging tree branch and the canoe capsized. Since then, she has paddled lakes and rivers from Temagami, Ontario, to the Boundary Waters of Minnesota. "For all that," she says, "I'm still better at soaking up the scenery from the bow of a canoe than steering a straight course from the stern." She is the editor of the Stories from Where We Live series, anthologies of literature from different regions of North America, and lives in Cambridge, Massachusetts, with her husband and two daughters.